ARTEK
SEVEN BRIDES FOR SEVEN ALIEN BROTHERS

HONEY PHILLIPS

Copyright © 2022 by Honey Phillips

All rights reserved. No part of this book may be used or reproduced by any means, graphic, electronic, or mechanical, including photocopying, recording, taping or by any information storage retrieval system without the written permission of the author.

Disclaimer

This book is a work of fiction. Names, characters, places, and incidents are products of the author's imagination or are used fictitiously and are not to be construed as real. Any resemblance to actual events, locales, organizations, or people, living or dead, is entirely coincidental.

Cover Design by Mariah Sinclair
Edited by Lindsay York at LY Publishing Services

❃ Created with Vellum

CHAPTER 1

Artek stood on a rocky outcropping overlooking the mountain valley and nodded with satisfaction at the ranch below. It had come a long way since they had arrived here two years ago. The herds of cattle grazing across the valley floor looked healthy and well fed. The fences had been repaired or replaced, even though keeping up with them was a daily chore. More food animals grazed on the lower slopes of the mountains, white dots from this distance, but he knew that they too were healthy and the size of the flock was increasing. The barns and stables had been repaired and were weather tight once more. The ranch house was still almost as decrepit as it had been when they arrived, but he and his men had slept in far worse. Still, it was time to begin on that project, especially if the idea he had been considering came to fruition.

The scrape of gravel made him tense, his hand automatically going to the weapon he still kept holstered at his hip, but he relaxed as the source of the disruption came into view. Callum, his former second-in-command, and a male he had known for almost his entire life. Callum had started out as his weapons tutor, but when the call came to serve, to protect their planet, Callum had not hesitated to follow Artek into combat. *Useless combat, as it turned out*, he thought bitterly, then shoved the thought away with the ease of long practice.

"Surveying the ranch?" Callum asked as he dismounted. The animal he was riding was called a horse—a hybrid developed by the humans who had also settled on this backwater planet. They were sturdy, usually placid animals, although they responded better to some of Artek's brothers than to others. This one, large enough to carry someone of Callum's substantial size, nudged noses with Artek's mount, then dropped his head to search for fodder amongst the rocks.

"I was seeing how far we have come over the past two years."

Callum nodded as he joined him. "I am satisfied, but there is still much to be done. We need to run irrigation ditches from the river to the fields. The fruit stock we planted is not doing as well as I would like. I will send Gilmat to take a look at it. And—"

"And the ranch house needs to be repaired," Artek interrupted.

Callum followed his glance to the sprawling, dilapidated building. It had been intended as a grand showplace by the original owner of the ranch, but that owner had retreated within its walls and let it fall to ruin long before they had purchased the ranch from his estate. Callum shrugged.

"We have lived in worse," he said, echoing Artek's previous thoughts.

"But it would not be suitable for a female."

Artek tried to keep his voice casual, but he wasn't entirely successful. Callum turned into a frozen statue next to him, but Artek waited patiently for him to speak. His second liked to consider matters first.

"We agreed on no females," Callum said at last.

"I know. When we arrived here, we were all tired and bitter. All of us wounded, even the ones whose wounds didn't show," he added.

Callum was one of those with unseen wounds. The losses they had experienced had chipped away at even the experienced warrior's normally stoic temperament.

Artek waited again, and finally Callum jerked his head in reluctant agreement.

"We have found a new life here. We have worked hard and are building a future." He looked directly at the other male. "I want to share that future with someone, with someone other than the six of you. I want a mate—a wife, as the humans say—and a child. Someone for whom to build this legacy."

He wasn't sure that he deserved that type of happiness, but he longed for it nonetheless and had finally decided to take the chance.

"I understand," Callum said finally. "But it will not be for me."

Artek didn't question him. He knew there had been a tragedy in his past life.

"I respect that. Can you respect my decision?"

Callum rubbed his temples, a weariness he did not usually show in the gesture.

"I can. But what about the others?"

"I'm not sure," he said honestly. "I suspect Drakkar will look down his nose at me and Gilmat will nod, then disappear into the greenhouse for hours. Benjar and Endark I think will be in favor. I suspect that they are both beginning to hunger for mates, although I do not think that either one of them knows how to woo a female."

"Especially a human female?" Callum asked, raising an eyebrow. "Since the only females anywhere close to us are humans, I assume you have a human bride in mind."

"I have been considering it." *Much more than just considering it.*

"And what of Frantor?"

Artek sighed. Frantor had been one of the ones to suffer the most wounds, both mental and physical. It had taken him months to stop hiding from his brothers in arms. Would he be able to cope with a strange face, especially a female face?

"I don't know. I hope that my bride might convince him that he is not as terrible as he thinks. As well as teach the younger males more... civilized behavior."

Callum nodded again, then shot him a penetrating look.

"Do you have someone in mind?"

"Yes." He did his best to keep his expression composed and his voice neutral. "I thought the shopkeeper's daughter, Nelly. She is a sensible female, and I believe she will be of great assistance in restoring the ranch house."

He didn't mention the fact that her face haunted his dreams and that he was becoming increasingly obsessed with knowing what lay beneath her shapeless clothing. Even her eyes fascinated him, changing from golden brown to green depending on her mood. From the hint of amusement on Callum's face, he suspected he had not been entirely successful in concealing his feelings.

Callum nodded gravely. "And not in the first flush of youth. She will undoubtedly be grateful for the offer."

"What do you mean by that? Any male would be lucky to have her."

His fists clenched at the insult to his female before he realized that Callum was raising an eyebrow again at his reaction.

"As I suspected. Have you spoken to her about this?"

"You know that we have had only the briefest interactions." Enough to know that she had a low, melodic voice that soothed his war stressed nerves. Enough to see the intelligence and humor in her eyes. Enough to feel the desire that simmered between them.

"Do you know whether or not she will be agreeable to your proposition?" Callum persisted.

"I don't know," he said honestly. "I do know that her male relative does not treat her with sufficient respect. And I suspect that she is not happy with her current life."

"And you think she would be happy here?" Callum's gesture embraced the entire ranch.

"I will make her happy," he said, more to himself than Callum.

The vow was so quiet that he wasn't sure that Callum even heard him, but a big hand descended on his shoulders.

"Then I suggest we talk to the others and prepare to make a trip to town."

CHAPTER 2

"What about Ferdie?" Nelly's father asked her.

She finished neatly stacking the bolts of fabric on the shelf, then turned to glare at him.

"Are you serious? He must be ten years younger than I am." She climbed down off the ladder and shook her head. "Besides, you know he's in love with Julie Watson. Not that I think he has a chance of making it past Mrs. Watson's expectations."

Or Julie's for that matter. During the brief conversations she'd had with the shy, enchantingly pretty girl, she had discovered that Julie was surprisingly well read and had an inquiring mind. Ferdie might be young and good looking enough to turn most girls' heads, but somehow she didn't think Julie was among them.

"He knows that," her father said. "That's why he's willing to put up with—"

He clamped his lips together, but it was too late. She narrowed her eyes at him.

"To put up with me, you mean? Well, don't worry. He won't have to. I have no intention of marrying him—or any other man in this town for that matter."

She stalked off behind the counter, doing her best to ignore the pinch of sadness hidden in her anger. It wasn't as if she was interested in Ferdie, but that he thought so little of her still stung a little. *Which is my own fault,* she admitted to herself. After an unfortunate experience with a suitor who turned out to be more interested in the store than in her, she had chosen her current disguise of shapeless clothes and tightly braided hair. No one ever seemed to look further. *And that's the way I like it.*

"Well, what about Desmond Potter?" her father asked, drumming his fingers anxiously on the counter. "He's in the market for a new wife."

She gave an exasperated huff. "Because he's already buried two."

"That wasn't his fault."

"Maybe not directly, but everyone knows that Sue Ellen died of pneumonia because he was too cheap to keep the house warm. And poor Lily was even worse. She just faded away, shut up in that big old house. I don't intend to let that happen to me."

Her father sighed, but didn't try to argue with her. Instead, he cast a longing look out at the street as two of his friends walked by, no doubt heading for the saloon.

"I think I'll go take a walk around town," he said. "See what's going on."

There was nothing going on. Just the same people following the same routines and exchanging the same gossip. But she didn't bother to contradict him.

"All right. I'll mind the store."

He nodded, still tapping his fingers on the counter and she put her hand over his.

"Cheer up, Pa. As long as I'm not married, I'm still here to look after things when you want to go for one of your walks."

"Miranda thinks we could get a clerk—" he blurted out, then flinched.

He undoubtedly expected her to snap at him again, but she managed to keep her face calm. The fact that Miranda was behind his latest push to marry her off didn't really surprise her. Her father had been courting the attractive widow for more than six months now, but she adamantly refused to marry him as long as Nelly was still running the store and living at home. Nelly couldn't even find it in her heart to blame the woman. She was pretty sure that if their positions had been reversed, she wouldn't have wanted to deal with her future husband's headstrong spinster daughter either.

She even thought that the widow would do a good job of keeping her father in check—there would be no wandering off to the saloon in the middle of the afternoon if Miranda were in charge. But despite that knowledge, and despite the fact that she loved her father and really did want him to be happy, she just couldn't bring herself to marry any of the men in town. The younger ones weren't interested, and the older ones had either been married before or she was all too aware of their faults.

Maybe I just missed my chance, she thought gloomily as she followed her father to the door. He headed off down the street, and she stood looking out at the town.

Wainwright was nestled at the base of the White Mountains, and their snow-capped peaks loomed protectively over the town. Josiah Wainwright had founded the town some fifty years ago, choosing this location for the fertile plains that stretched out in the other direction—and for its isolated position.

Born into an immensely wealthy family, his parents' unexpected demise had left him in sole charge of the family business. Obsessed with the idea of a simpler time, he had been determined to leave an overcrowded and polluted Earth behind and create a new life on Cresca. He had purchased the land on which the town was built along with a vast amount of surrounding acreage and then offered the opportunity to homestead the land to anyone who worked in his businesses. Many of them jumped at the chance to leave Earth behind, despite the hard work that would be required.

Two ships full of settlers had accompanied Josiah to Cresca. After overseeing the construction of the town, Josiah had set about building his own home on a vast ranch nestled deep in the mountains. The home had been built in preparation for his bride, but the bride never came. Town legend was divided on whether she had simply refused to abandon her comfortable life on Earth or if she had died before she could join him.

Whatever the truth of the matter, Josiah had turned into a recluse, barely appearing in town and showing little interest in helping the settlers find the new life he had promised them. At least when he died, all of the land and buildings on this side of the mountain had been bequeathed to the current owners and residents. His own ranch had been sold, although it had taken over a year to find anyone willing to take on the hard work and isolated location.

But none of the townspeople had expected the current occupants. Nelly could still remember the arguments that had taken place at a hastily called town meeting two years ago.

"This can't be legal," old Mr. Wilson protested. "They're aliens. Soldiers. They could just decide to sweep in here and take over."

"That seems most unlikely," Pearl said quietly. She was a sensible woman, a few years older than Nelly, and still wearing black from her recent widowhood.

"Oh yeah? You say that now. What if they come sniffing after that pretty little sister of yours?" Tom Cole demanded.

Pearl's lips drew together for a moment, but Nelly suspected that her friend was more worried that her sister would be the interested party. Ruby had a flirtatious nature that was going to get her in trouble one of these days.

"I am quite capable of looking after my sister," Pearl said firmly. "I would assume that all of you are equally capable of looking after your daughters... and your wives."

Outraged shouts followed and Nelly did her best to hide her smile.

"I just don't like it," Mr. Briggs said ponderously. He was what passed for a legal representative in their small town and had a vastly inflated sense of his own importance. "Perhaps we can still stop the transaction?"

Mr. Purvis, the banker, pursed his lips together disapprovingly. "The transaction has already been completed. And may I remind you, gentlemen... and ladies, we did discuss purchasing the ranch for the town and no one was willing to proceed."

Another round of accusations broke out. Nelly heard the word *alien* so many times that she finally snapped. Ignoring her father's attempt to stop her, she rose from her seat.

"You all keep talking about *aliens*, but I think you are forgetting something. This isn't Earth. This isn't our planet. We are all aliens here. And they have as much right to be here as we do."

That was, of course, not the end of the matter, but she didn't stay to hear anymore. She left the meeting, and Pearl followed her out.

"They'll never accept them, you know," Pearl said quietly.

"I know. But then they barely accept me."

The other woman smiled at her, and they walked in silence for a few minutes before Nelly looked at her.

"Are you worried about your sister?"

Pearl sighed. "Always. She's so anxious for excitement. For her life to begin, as she puts it." A shadow crossed her face. "I wish I could make her understand that growing up isn't always pleasant."

Nelly touched her friend's shoulder. Pearl's husband Marcus had been a cruel man, and she suspected that Pearl suffered during the marriage, although she never complained.

"We don't even know what these so-called aliens look like," she said lightly, hoping to erase that shadow. "They probably won't appeal to us at all."

She was wrong.

A month later, the bell over the store's entrance tinkled and she looked up to see the most striking male she'd ever seen. His shoulders were broad enough to fill the doorway, and the spiraling horns atop his head made him duck as he entered. He was dressed in a faded grey uniform, neatly pressed despite its age, and he walked towards her with the firm confidence of a warrior. Aside from the uniform, everything about him was blue—from smooth blue skin to short midnight blue hair to those impressive horns. In contrast, his eyes were a rich golden yellow, and when they met hers, she felt as if all the air had left the room.

They stared at each other for what felt like an eternity before his companion cleared his throat and broke the spell. She gave the other male a brief glance—he also had horns but they curled back and down, and his skin was a rich purple. Obviously from another species, he looked older, the dark hair at his temples turning grey, but he carried himself with that same easy confidence.

When she looked back at the first male, his face had frozen into a stern mask and whatever connection she thought she'd felt had disappeared.

"I am Commander... I am Artek," he amended. "I wish to purchase these items."

He handed her a list, and as he did, their fingers touched. She felt that brief contact as if a spark of electricity had run through her body, but she did her best to mirror his own stoic expression as she studied the contents of the list.

"I have some of these items in stock. These I can get from Williamsburg. Most of the mechanical equipment will need to come from Port Cantor, and it will take some time."

He frowned, and she watched in fascination as his horns grew closer together.

"Is there any way to expedite them?"

She shook her head. "I'm afraid not. It's simply a supply-chain issue. The rail line only goes as far as Williamsburg. Everything is brought by wagon from there."

"There is no air transportation?" the other male asked.

"Nothing that will cover this distance. Outside of the major ports, it is too difficult to maintain mechanical vehicles. Hiring one from Port Cantor would easily cost three times the cost of the actual goods."

"Very well," Artek said. "Please make arrangements for those items to be delivered using the standard methods. We will begin with what you have here."

"Adapt and survive," the other male said softly, and Artek nodded.

To her surprise, as she began gathering their supplies, both males came to assist her. Most of her customers preferred to stand at the counter and let her wait on them. She almost wished these two had done the same. She became increasingly aware of Artek—of the muscles in his arms bulging as he pulled down a crate of canned goods, of the way the fabric of his uniform tightened across his buttocks as he bent down and picked up a barrel and then heaved it easily onto a broad shoulder. And every time he passed by her, she was conscious of a delicious spicy fragrance and the warmth of his body. Only long years of practice kept her from showing her reaction. He would have no interest in a plain human shopkeeper.

When they completed loading their wagon, he tried to hand her a credit chit for the entire amount.

"You don't need to pay for the other items until they arrive," she said.

He frowned again. "But what if you order the items and I don't purchase them when they arrive? It does not seem fair to you."

"It wouldn't be the first time it's happened," she said dryly.

"It will not happen this time."

He handed her the credit chit again, and this time she took it. Once again, their hands brushed and that jolt of energy swept over her. Grateful that her clothes were baggy enough to hide the fact that her nipples had hardened, she turned away to process the transaction. When she turned back, he was still looking down at his hand.

"Is there a way to contact you? To let you know when everything arrives," she added hastily.

He shook his head.

"No." After a brief hesitation, he added, "We will return in six weeks."

His eyes returned to her face, gold once more, before he nodded and left abruptly. She was still staring at the doorway when her father hurried in a few minutes later.

"Nelly! I heard those aliens were here. You didn't sell anything to them, did you?"

"Of course I did."

"But—"

"Pa, you know as well as I do that we can't afford to turn away business."

"But what if they can't pay?"

"Unlike some of your personal friends, they didn't try to open an account. They paid for everything, including their upcoming deliveries."

He stared at her in dismay.

"You mean they're coming back?"

I hope so.

"Yes," she said coldly. "And we will sell to them."

And they did come back. Artek and his silent partner, who she eventually discovered was named Callum, came every six weeks until the winter snows closed the pass. And every time, she grew more and more fascinated by him.

Now the snow on the mountain peaks reminded her that the pass would soon close again, and all she'd have to look forward to was a long, dreary winter. Sighing, she took out a duster and started cleaning the shelves.

But her mind was not on her chores. She was still thinking about Artek when the door opened and he walked in.

CHAPTER 3

*A*rtek reached for the shop door, then hesitated as the familiar doubts swept over him.

"Are you reconsidering?" Callum asked.

"No," he said resolutely and opened the door.

As he walked inside he found his heart rate increasing, almost as if he were preparing for battle. *Don't be ridiculous*, he told himself. *Consider it a business transaction. If she refuses...*

His thoughts stopped at that point. He couldn't imagine another alternative if she refused. Perhaps in the spring he should visit one of the larger cities. The thought did not give him any pleasure. Business transaction or not, this was the female who he wanted as his partner.

Looking around for Nelly, he found her standing next to the tall cabinets that lined both sides of the store, a dust cloth in her hand. Whenever he visited she was always working. Her father did not seem to play any role in actually managing the store. Yet another reason why she would be better off with him.

"Commander Artek. I didn't expect you... I mean, you're not scheduled to return for another two weeks."

Her face remained composed, but he saw the faintest hint of pink on her cheeks. The change of color was so slight that another person might not have noticed, but over the past two summers he'd learned to detect every subtle change in her expression.

"I wish to speak with you," he said, then had to fight to keep his own face composed. The words came out more as a command than a request.

"All right. Was there a problem with your last order?"

"No. This isn't about our supplies. It's about a different kind of... transaction."

Her brows drew together in an unexpectedly charming look of confusion.

"I don't understand. Is there something else you wish for me to arrange?"

Before he could decide how to continue, the bell over the shop door rang again and two females entered. A plump female a few years older than his female, accompanied by a wide-eyed younger one. The older woman looked startled, but not afraid, and the girl's gaze was frankly appraising. She gave them both a teasing smile, and he realized she was older than she first appeared.

"How nice to see some new... men," the girl giggled. "I'm Ruby."

She took a step towards them before the older female grabbed her arm.

"Sorry to interrupt you while you're busy, Nelly. We'll come back later."

As she turned to guide the girl back to the door, Callum stepped forward to open it for her. Their bodies collided for the briefest instant, Callum pausing for just a second before steadying the older female and immediately stepping back. She gave him a flustered look, her cheeks turning pink, before she hurried the girl out of the store ignoring her protests.

"Is there somewhere else we could talk?" he asked, already anticipating another interruption.

"I'm afraid not. I don't have anyone else to watch over the store—"

"I can do that," Callum's deep voice interrupted.

"You?" Nelly gave him a doubtful look. "I'm not sure if—"

"Your prices are clearly labeled on each of the items you carry in stock. The price list for anything which needs to be ordered is listed in the book next to your accounting machine. The machine is used for cash transactions, and credit transactions are made on the datapad. It is a simple process." Callum gave her a direct look. "Unless you do not trust me?"

"Of course not..." She paused, then smiled at his second in a way that Artek did not appreciate. "Actually, I trust you more than most of the people here in town. If you don't mind watching over things for a few minutes, I'm happy to let you take over. Does that work, Commander?"

"Call me Artek," he said as he had many times before. "Is there a suitable location at the back of the store? I am afraid that a more public location would draw attention."

A flash of amusement crossed her face. "I'm quite sure about that. Come with me."

She turned and led the way through the door behind the counter, her movements graceful despite the voluminous gown she was wearing. The door opened into a small storage room, but she continued through it to a larger space with cooking equipment along one wall, a sturdy wooden table on the other, and a seating area at the rear overlooking an enclosed garden area. Everything was spotlessly clean and neat.

Her eyes widened when she turned and found him right behind her. Something flickered in those changeable eyes, but before he could analyze it, she headed for the rear door.

"Let's talk outside."

All three sides of the garden were edged with neat planting boxes, still full of late-blooming plants and the last of the summer vegetables. Another table and chairs sat in the middle of the space, but neither one of them sat.

"It's a beautiful day," she murmured, looking up at the sky. "I'm not sure how much longer we're going to be enjoying this warm weather."

"No, winter is coming," he agreed, and then stood in awkward silence for a moment. Why was he finding this so unexpectedly difficult?

She moved over to one of the beds and began breaking off dead leaves with her usual quick, graceful movements.

"What was it you wanted to ask me about?"

"You know that my brothers and I purchased Josiah Wainwright's ranch," he said, then cursed himself for being an idiot. Of course she knew.

"Your brothers?"

"We consider ourselves brothers. Our bond was forged in... difficult times." She did not need to know just how difficult that war had been for all of them. "We have been working together on restoring the ranch. We have made a great deal of progress, but it needs a... female influence."

Her hand stilled on the plant, but he couldn't see her face.

"Yes?" Her voice was low, cautious.

"I would like you to be that female and move to the ranch with me. As my wife," he added hastily, wanting to make sure that she understood his intentions were honorable.

"Why me?"

Her voice was still cautious, and she still wasn't looking at him. He wanted to take her by the shoulders and turn her around to face him, but he was afraid that once he touched her his restraint might disappear.

"I believe you to be a sensible, intelligent female."

His voice sounded stilted even in his own ears, and her shoulders seemed to droop.

"There are other women who fit those requirements," she said quietly.

"Not as far as I'm concerned."

That brought her head around, the sunlight catching sparks of green fire in her eyes.

"You want me?"

"I am not interested in another female. You would also receive an equal share in the ranch," he added, hoping that would help sway her in his favor.

She didn't seem to be listening, her eyes still focused on his face.

"But just me?"

"Yes."

A slow smile brightened her face, as if the sun had emerged from behind a cloud, and then she nodded.

"In that case, I agree to your proposal."

A dizzying wave of relief rushed over him. She had accepted him.

Remembering the human custom for sealing a bargain, he hesitated then carefully extended his hand. She also hesitated, but then she reached out and took it. Triumph roared through him. He had her.

CHAPTER 4

𝒩elly stared at their clasped hands, her small fingers almost lost in his much larger ones, and tried not to panic. She'd never expected to celebrate her engagement with a handshake.

It's not too late.

But her sensible inner voice was drowned out by the flood of warmth filling her body from that simple contact. When she looked up, Artek's eyes were glowing golden yellow again, and that reassured her. In the end, it had been the way they responded to each other, as well as the hint of vulnerability on his face when he said that he was only interested in her that had made her decide to accept his proposal. She knew it was impulsive, possibly reckless, but she was tired of watching life pass her by. It was time for a change, and Artek would most certainly be a change.

"An engagement is usually celebrated with a kiss," she told him.

"A kiss?"

Oh. She hadn't expected him not to know about kissing. Just how much was she going to have to explain to him?

"It's when our mouths touch. It's a gesture of... affection."

His eyes immediately focused on her mouth, the heat in them increasing.

"A kiss," he repeated, but this time his voice was deep and growly.

"Yes. Bend your head towards me."

He obeyed, and she braced her hand on one wide shoulder then lifted up enough to press her lips against his. The simmering attraction between them flared, and she could feel a heavy pulse between her legs. She waited expectantly, but he simply stood there, their mouths pressed together.

Telling herself she was not disappointed, she dropped back down to her feet.

"I suppose we should go and relieve Callum from his duties and begin making the arrangements. When do you want to get married?"

His fingers were pressed to his mouth, and he had the strangest look on his face, but eventually her question seemed to penetrate and he stood upright, assuming his usual military stiffness.

"Today."

"Today? I'm not sure I can—"

Or could she? As much as she would have preferred more time to prepare, perhaps even to have Becky sew her wedding dress and some more attractive clothes, this was not a romantic union. And the less time her father had to think of objections, the better.

"I think that could be arranged," she amended. "Especially if Callum could watch the store for a little while longer. He seems very capable."

"I am equally capable," he said stiffly, and she realized she had offended him.

She put a cautious hand on his arm, tempted to linger over all that warm, hard muscle.

"I'm sure you are, but you will need to see Mr. Madison to arrange for the license and the ceremony." And wouldn't he be shocked? She wished she could be there to see the look on the man's usually placid face.

"Do you think he will object?"

"Maybe, but don't give him a chance to argue. And I guess I should tell my father."

"I will do that," he said firmly. "It is a human husband's duty to discuss the marriage with the female's male relative," he added when she looked up at him curiously.

The fact that he had bothered to find out about human customs was even more reassuring, and she gave his arm a little squeeze before reluctantly removing her hand.

"Then let's go and ask Callum to stay for another hour."

"He will stay."

"Because you're his commander?"

"No, because he is my friend— my brother."

A lump appeared in her throat. How much she envied that familial relationship. She wasn't even sure she could count on her father to come to the wedding, and the few friends she had in town would be working. She would ask Pearl to accompany her, she decided as they returned to the store.

She groaned as she reentered the store and saw Mr. Elam scurrying out through the door. He was one of her father's friends and seemed to think that entitled him to unlimited credit.

"How much did he want to charge this time?" she asked Callum.

"He wanted a bottle of the imported whiskey," he said, and she winced. It was one of their most expensive items.

"But I did not allow him to purchase any," Callum continued.

"You didn't? Why not?"

"Because he already owes too much money to your business. Instead, he made a small payment on his account. Too small," he added, frowning. "But he assured me that was all he had available."

Her eyes widened. "You actually made Mr. Elam make a payment?"

"Was that wrong? The amount of debt seemed unreasonable considering his failure to repay."

"No, that's wonderful. You are doing an excellent job of minding the store."

When she smiled at him, Artek made an odd growling noise and stepped up next to her.

"We are getting married."

Callum nodded solemnly. "As I anticipated."

Why had he anticipated it? Was she so obviously interested?

Before she could decide, Artek continued.

"I must arrange for the ceremony and notify Nelly's father. She also needs time to prepare. We need you to remain in charge here."

"If that's all right with you," she added hastily.

"Of course."

"I will return within the hour," Artek said, turning to look down at her.

He hesitated, then bent down and once again pressed his lips against hers before straightening and marching out of the store. This time, she was the one left pressing her fingers against her tingling lips.

"He's very decisive," she murmured.

"He is when he wants to accomplish something."

She looked over to find Callum studying her.

"Do you object?"

He shook his head. "We voted, and we all agreed to offer you a share in our partnership."

That sounded more clinical than she had anticipated.

"So you were expecting him to bring back a bride?"

"Not a bride, you. He was not interested in any other female."

The smile escaped before she could call it back.

"I'm glad. But now I'd better get going. I don't want to be late."

"I believe you have arrived just in time."

She suspected that Callum was referring to much more than the wedding ceremony, and she gave him a grateful smile before heading to the door.

Exactly an hour later, she stood outside the door to Mr. Madison's office, trying to calm her racing heart. Artek and Callum were already inside waiting for her. To her surprise, her father was at her side. A few minutes after she returned from Pearl's, he'd entered the store, red-faced and panting.

"That alien says you're going to marry him," he huffed out. "Just came into the saloon and said *I'm marrying your daughter*, then turned around and walked out. Who the hell does he think he is?"

She did her best to hide her smile. Apparently, Artek's interpretation of human customs was not entirely accurate.

"That's because I am marrying him," she said calmly.

"But you can't! They're aliens..." His voice trailed off as he finally noticed Callum, standing tall and forbidding behind the cash register, and she saw him gulp. "I mean..."

"We are all aliens on this planet," Callum said, echoing her words from that original town meeting as he moved out from behind the counter. "Since your father has returned, I will go and find the commander. We will meet you at the registry office."

"Thanks again, Callum."

He inclined his head as he headed for the door, then paused. "I collected two additional overdue payments while you were gone. They have been entered into your account book."

She laughed. "Then I'm doubly thankful. I'll see you at the ceremony."

As soon as the bell tinkled behind him, her father turned on her.

"Nelly, you can't do this. Don't you understand?"

"I thought you wanted me to get married," she said lightly.

"I do, but not like this. I shudder to think what Miranda is going to have to say about it."

"My guess is that she'll be thrilled," she said dryly, but his expression didn't lighten. "Pa, I really think this is best for all of us. You know I've never been a particularly good fit here in town. This is a chance for a different life. And I won't be that far away."

He heaved a heavy sigh, then gave a reluctant nod.

"I guess it's not much worse than you marrying someone on one of those distant farms. If only he were human..."

"Well, he's not." She hesitated again. "I'd like you to come to the ceremony. Will you do that?"

"But the store..."

Despite his protests, when it came time to leave, he'd been waiting for her. He'd even slicked back his hair and put on his Sunday suit.

"Thank you, Pa," she said softly, kissing his cheek.

He sniffed and blew his nose on a big red spotted handkerchief.

"You look just like your Ma in that dress."

The outfit was one of Pearl's, hastily tucked in to accommodate her more slender figure, but it was far nicer than anything she had worn in a very long time. The white lace collar framed her face, and the pretty gathered blouse was buttoned into a dark skirt that fell smoothly down over her hips to a flounce at the bottom. She felt... pretty.

"Thank you," she whispered, her voice shaking as she took his arm.

And now here they were. A battery of curious eyes had watched them as he escorted her down the sidewalk and into the registrar's office, but no one said anything. Pearl was the only one waiting for her, and she smiled and handed her a small bouquet of late summer roses.

"Here. Every bride should have a bouquet."

Afraid she might burst into tears, she bent over and sniffed the sweet fragrance. When she recovered her composure, she gave her friend a curious look.

"Ruby didn't come with you?"

"She isn't back yet, thank goodness. You know she would be beside herself with excitement, and this should be your day. Are you ready?"

"I'm ready," she said firmly, and Pearl opened the door.

CHAPTER 5

*A*rtek had his eyes fixed on the door as it opened. He had been doing his best to stand patiently, despite the fear that Nelly might change her mind and not show up. And then she was there, beautiful enough to take his breath away. Her hair had been released from its usual braid to cascade down next to her face and the late afternoon sunlight streaming into the office struck red sparks in the dark waves. Her outfit was different as well, and even though it covered her completely, it revealed far more of her supple figure than he had even seen before.

His shaft threatened to escape his control, and he had the sudden urge to forget about the ceremony and carry her off as one of his primitive ancestors might have done. Instead, he took a deep breath and smiled at her.

She returned his smile, then came towards him with her usual quick, graceful steps and the familiarity of her movements steadied him. When she reached him, he took her hand just as he had done earlier, and her small fingers already felt right in his grasp.

The officiant cleared his throat nervously. He was a plump, red-faced male, and his hand shook as he adjusted his small gold spectacles.

"Umm, are there any objections to this union?"

Artek growled, and the male gave him a pleading look.

"It's part of the ceremony. I have to ask. Mr. Armstrong?"

The question was directed at Nelly's father, but although he scowled, he shook his head.

"Then, uh, let us begin."

The ceremony did not last long, but he meant every word of his vows. Nelly looked equally solemn as she repeated her own portion.

The officiant looked relieved as the short ceremony came to a conclusion.

"I now pronounce you man and—"

"I am not a man," he interrupted. "I am a Kemberian."

The male coughed nervously.

"Err, well, yes, but those are the words."

"I do not care. I wish to make sure that the words are accurate so that there can be no doubt about the legitimacy of the ceremony." He did not intend to take any chances on losing Nelly now that he had her.

ARTEK

"If you insist." The officiant pushed his glasses up his nose again. "I now pronounce you Kemberian and wife. You may kiss the bride."

He wasn't sure he understood this human obsession with kissing. It was certainly a pleasant experience to feel Nelly's soft lips beneath his, but there were other places on her body he was far more interested in exploring with his mouth. However, it seemed to be expected, so he put his arm around her waist and drew her close before bending down to kiss her. He rejoiced in the feel of her body against his and the gentle press of her lips.

He could hardly wait until he had her alone. He was already considering the first place he wished to explore when her lips parted slightly beneath his and her tongue flicked shyly at the seam of his mouth. Startled, his own lips parted and her tongue slipped into his mouth, soft and wet and unspeakably provocative. Her sweet taste exploded in his mouth, and desire rushed over him so quickly that he almost swayed. He pulled her closer, pressing that strong supple body against his as he finally understood just what it meant to kiss his wife.

"Commander."

Only the sound of Callum's voice finally penetrated enough for him to raise his head. Nelly looked up at him, her eyes wide and dark and her lips pink and swollen. She looked delicious and he wanted to demand more of these kisses, but they were not yet alone.

Callum was waiting patiently, his face as impenetrable as usual, although Artek knew him well enough to see the glint of amusement in his eyes. Nelly's father was red-faced and glaring while the officiant nervously shuffled his papers. Only the other female smiled at the pair of them.

"I didn't have time to prepare much, but I have wine and cakes waiting at my house for a small celebration," she said.

Before he could refuse, Nelly returned her smile.

"That sounds very nice, Pearl. Thank you."

He bit back his instinctive protest. She was his now—this delay would not change that.

"Won't you join us, Mr. Armstrong? I have some of my special pear brandy as well."

Nelly's father finally stopped glaring at him long enough to nod.

"I reckon I could use a drink."

The officiant quickly declined his invitation and the five of them exited his offices. More than the usual number of townspeople cluttered the street, their attempts to look as though they were simply going about their daily business unconvincing at best. He kept alert for any signs of trouble, but they appeared shocked rather than aggressive and he decided to ignore them.

Pearl's house was of an impressive size, set back from the street behind a pretty garden. While it was still smaller than the ranch house, unlike their house it looked neat and well cared for. He saw Callum look at the house and thought he saw resignation on his friend's face before he opened the gate for Pearl. She didn't look up at him as she entered, but from the color tinting her cheeks, he suspected she was far from oblivious.

But unlike Callum, he had claimed his bride and Nelly smiled up at him as they entered the house together. The inside was as neat and pretty as the outside, but it was not an environment suited to males and even Nelly's father looked uncomfortable as he perched on the edge of a delicate sofa and drank rapidly from a glass filled with clear liquid.

The conversation was stilted at best, and he tried not to reveal his impatience, even though his body was practically vibrating with the need to claim his female. After the fifth time the conversation ended in an awkward silence, he could stand it no longer.

"It is time to leave," he said, rising to his feet and holding out his hand for Nelly.

"Leave?" She bit her lip. "I hadn't thought... That is, do we have time to make it back to the ranch tonight before dark? I still have packing to do."

"We are not returning to the ranch tonight. I have arranged another location for our..." What was the human expression? "Our sweet moon."

She gave him a puzzled look, then smiled. "Do you mean a honeymoon?"

"Is that the correct expression?"

"If you mean what I think you do. But where are we going?"

He hesitated. He had intended to surprise her with his arrangements.

"Do you trust me?"

Those small sparks of green lit her eyes as she nodded.

"I do."

"Well, I don't," her father said, staggering to his feet. "I want to know where you're taking my girl."

He was tempted to tell the man that it was no longer his concern, but he did not want to upset his new bride.

"It is not far. We will return in the morning so that Nelly can collect her belongings and say goodbye."

"But what about tonight?" she asked. "I should at least stop and get a nightgown and a few other things."

"You do not need clothing tonight," he said firmly, ignoring her father's outraged gasp. "Now come with me. Please," he added, holding out his hand again.

She bit her lip again, but to his immense satisfaction, she took his hand and let him pull her to her feet.

"Thank you for your hospitality," he said to the other female as he tugged his bride out of the room.

"Yes, thank you, Pearl," Nelly said breathlessly as he walked quickly out of the house and down the street. "Can you slow down a little, Artek?"

"Of course. Forgive my impatience. I just wish to be alone with you. And my legs are longer than yours. Perhaps I should carry you."

"You'll do no such thing. We have enough people watching us already."

She was correct. The number of curious onlookers had not lessened.

"Cover your ears," he told her.

She frowned, but obeyed. As soon as she did, he turned back towards the street and roared, a deep, echoing growl that rolled along the main street. The people who had been watching flinched, then suddenly found reasons to return to their homes or business establishments.

"I can't believe you did that," she said, looking at the now empty street.

"Do you object?"

"No. There are several times in the past where that would have come in very useful." She smiled up at him and stepped a little closer. "You are a man—a Kemberian—of hidden talents."

An unexpected warmth went through him at her praise, but he did his best to ignore it.

"May I carry you now that we are no longer under observation?"

"They may not be on the street, but I'm sure they're still peeping through the windows. And besides, I don't mind walking."

He escorted her to the next intersection, then turned towards the edge of town. Their destination was a small wooden building at the end of the street. It was the last building, with nothing beyond it but the lower slopes of the mountains.

"I had forgotten this was here," she said as they reached it. "Isn't this the office that Josiah had built to handle ranch business here in town?"

"That's correct. It was included in the estate."

"But it must have been empty for years."

"Not at all. We have been using it when our visits to town required an overnight stay."

"And this is where we're going to spend our honeymoon?"

He could hear the doubt in her voice, but he hoped that his understanding of human customs had been correct and that his arrangements would please her. He stepped up onto the shallow porch that lined the front of the building and opened the door, then returned to pick her up.

"You cannot object to this. It is a husband's right to carry his wife across the threshold."

She smiled at him, their faces only inches apart, and the delights of her mouth an almost unbearable temptation.

"No, I don't object."

He carried her into the building and shut the door firmly behind them.

CHAPTER 6

Nelly's heart pounded as Artek carried her into the building. His enthusiasm both delighted and terrified her. All through the ceremony and the modest celebration, she had been conscious of him, of his warm, strong body and his delicious scent. But she was also quite aware of the fact that he wasn't human—and that she might not understand his thoughts and expectations.

She was so busy thinking about those expectations that it took her a moment to look around their surroundings. Her racing thoughts finally slowed as she looked around. The interior of the building was undeniably rustic, but he had made every attempt to transform it. Two sturdy wooden bed frames had been pushed together to form one large bed, the mattresses covered with a pristine white sheet. Her pulse jumped at the sight of the bed and the thought of what would occur there.

Flower petals were scattered across the sheet, and more flowers were arranged in small bouquets placed around the room. One of them stood on the table which had been neatly covered with a colorful cloth. She recognized the basket next to it as coming from Florie's restaurant. Although the room was equipped with an overhead light, candles waited atop the table and on the shelves next to the bed. They were unlit since the last of the afternoon sunlight still slanted into the room, but it was a thoughtful gesture.

"I can't believe you got all of this done in an hour," she said softly, moving over to the table and stroking one of the flowers that made up the bouquet. Late-summer roses, just like those in her wedding bouquet, and she added them to the arrangement.

"I made some preparations before I came to speak to you."

"You did? Were you so sure of me?"

"No. My heart pounded as if I were going into battle before I entered the store."

His answer soothed her and helped calm her fears, but her pulse was still beating wildly. An awkward silence fell, and she finally put her hand on the basket.

"Are you hungry? Would you like something to eat?"

"I am not hungry for food."

He was still standing by the door, his body rigid, but his eyes were glowing that rich golden yellow again. She felt a betraying warmth in her own cheeks as she went to the window and began pulling the faded curtains closed.

"Why are you doing that? I wish to see you."

"Then why don't you light the candles? I don't want anyone looking in on us."

Not that she really expected anyone would be foolish enough or improper enough to try, but she felt exposed with the windows uncovered.

"Callum will remain on watch."

That made her hesitate, peering cautiously through the window. "He's going to stay outside? All night?"

"It is considered an honor amongst my people." A hint of humor relieved the stern mask. "Do not worry. He will be close, but not too close."

Her cheeks heated again as she moved to the next window. By the time she had finished closing the curtains, he had the candles lit. The flickering light made the room feel warm and intimate, as if the two of them were enclosed in their own private bubble.

He was standing by the table now, his body still rigid, and she gave him an uncertain look. Despite his impatience to be alone with her, he now seemed reluctant to actually touch her. Or could it be that he was nervous as well? A thought suddenly occurred to her as she remembered his inexperience with kissing.

"Are you a virgin?" she blurted out.

"Of course not. I have been instructed in how to please a female," he said stiffly.

"A human female?"

"No, but I have no doubt that I can please you."

His voice had deepened to a low growl that sent a pleasant shiver up her spine. Gathering her courage, she gave him a provocative look.

"How would you do that?"

"I would begin by removing your clothing. And then I would kiss you. I enjoy kissing you very much."

She shivered again as she remembered the way he had kissed her after the ceremony—the urgency of his mouth and the way it had awoken a corresponding hunger in her own body.

"I would kiss your breasts and the sweetness between your legs. And when you were wet and ready, I would mount you and make you my mate. My wife."

Oh, Lord. Her nipples tightened into stiff little buds beneath her blouse, and that warm, heavy ache was back between her thighs. Her fingers trembled as she raised them to the top button of her blouse, and he growled.

"I said I would remove your clothing."

He stalked towards her, huge and powerful, the candlelight flickering in the spiraling ridges of his horns, and her heart pounded. Everything about him screamed strength and power, but his fingers were exquisitely gentle as he began to unbutton her blouse. He carefully unfastened each of the small pearl buttons, his hands warm and hard and tempting as he made his way down to her waist, and gently pulled the blouse free.

"It fastens at the wrists as well," she whispered, holding out her arms.

He undid those buttons as well and the blouse whispered to the ground behind her. Her skirt followed, leaving her clad only in her corset and chemise. He ran a finger slowly along the swell of her breasts above the low neckline and she shivered under the tantalizing touch.

"I have often wondered what lay beneath your clothing. Why do you hide such beauty?"

"Maybe I wanted a man who could see there was more to me than just my body."

His eyes stopped following the path of his finger and lifted her face.

"You have been hurt."

It was not a question, but she answered him anyway.

"Yes. There was someone who was only interested in my body —and the fact that my father owned the store."

"Foolish male. Would you like me to teach him the... error of his ways?"

The threat in his voice was quite clear, and she smiled up at him.

"No, thank you. And he moved away a long time ago."

"I would be happy to track him down."

"I would rather have you here." Gathering her courage, she pushed the strap of her chemise down over her shoulder. "Are you going to remove the rest?"

He growled an assent, but she had to show him how to unfasten the hooks down the front of the corset.

"Human clothing is very complicated."

"It doesn't have to be this complicated, but Josiah was obsessed with Earth's past. He thought it was a simpler and better time. He specified his idea of appropriate clothing in the guidelines when he founded the town."

"But he is no longer alive," he murmured absently, concentrating on each tiny hook.

Only the thin cotton of her chemise separated his hands from her skin, and she had to force herself to focus on her reply.

"It is a small town, and we have become very set in our ways. This is the way of life I know."

"Have you ever—"

Whatever he had intended to ask died away as he released the last hook and the corset dropped to the ground. The thin cotton beneath concealed almost nothing, and he growled his approval as his big hands reached up to cup her breasts. Her nipples were so hard they ached, and she pressed them eagerly into that warm, firm grip. He made an impatient sound, and then even her chemise was gone, ripped apart with almost terrifying ease. A fresh rush of heat swept through her body as his hands immediately returned to her breasts, and yes, it was so much better with nothing separating them.

"Now that you've undressed me, do I get to do the same?" she whispered.

"Not this time. I do not believe I would be able to remain in control."

His hand lingered a moment longer before he stepped back. He rapidly stripped off his uniform coat, flinging it to one side. The tight-fitting shirt he'd been wearing beneath it followed immediately, leaving a broad expanse of bare chest, his muscles rippling beneath that gleaming blue skin. She was still admiring the sight when he toed off his boots and removed his pants.

His cock sprang out between them, long and hard and... not human. The thick, dark blue shaft was covered with raised ridges in an intricate swirling pattern. Fascinated, she touched one of the ridges with a cautious finger. Hard and slightly rough, it seemed to pulse beneath her finger, but he growled and moved her hand away before she had a chance to explore.

"You will make me lose control."

A small pearl of liquid had appeared at the end of the thick shaft. Giving into temptation, she brushed her finger across it then lifted her damp finger to her mouth. Mmm, salty but also sweet. She licked her lips.

"Nelly," he groaned.

"Yes?"

"I have a plan. I have undressed you, and now I will kiss you, and then I will—"

"I remember. But I'm already wet and ready," she whispered, giddy with excitement.

His rigid control finally snapped as he lifted her into his arms and carried her to bed.

CHAPTER 7

Artek had Nelly stretched out on the bed and his cock at her entrance before a lingering remnant of control enabled him to pause. The sweet scent of her arousal filled his head and the wet kiss of her flesh against his cock tested him, but the dark length of his cock looked enormous against her soft pink flesh and he forced himself to remain still. But then her legs came up to circle his hips, urging him on, and that thread of control snapped. He sank into her body in one hard, wet stroke. She cried out, her body arching so violently that she almost dislodged.

He could feel her channel fluttering around him, the soft little pulses urging him on, but once again he managed to stop.

"Nelly? Are you all right?"

"Yes... No... So full..."

The words came out between rapid breaths as her head tossed back and forth on the pillow. A fine sheen of perspiration covered her skin, making her body glow in the candlelight, her nipples dark red and swollen.

"Perhaps I should..." He started to withdraw, but her body seemed to cling to his. His cock brushed across a place inside her that made her cry out again, and then she was climaxing, milking his shaft in hard, rhythmic pulses and destroying any hope of control.

He roared, gripping her hips to hold her in place as he thrust wildly into the welcoming depths of her body. Everything he had learned about pleasing a female disappeared beneath the urgent need to claim her as his mate and fill her with his seed. Fire raced down his spine, and then he too was coming in long endless bursts as he gathered her close.

"You caused me to abandon my plan," he murmured when his breathing finally slowed.

"I know. I kind of enjoyed seeing you lose control." She gave him a shy smile, the green flaring in her eyes. "It was exciting."

"It was dangerous. You don't know what I am capable of doing."

Her eyes grew darker as she gave him a thoughtful look, and then raised her hand to his cheek.

"I'm not afraid of you. I think—I know—that you would never hurt me."

Unable to speak, he bent his head and kissed her. The kiss started off sweet and gentle, but the need was still there, only partially sated by his previous release, and the intensity grew until she was clinging to him, rocking her hips against his. This time, he had enough control not to respond immediately.

"Now we will proceed according to my plan," he said, when he finally raised his head.

"We don't have to," she said, moving restlessly beneath him.

"I promised you I would pleasure you."

"You do. You did."

"And I intend to do so again. Completely, this time."

Ignoring her muffled protest, he lowered his mouth to her breasts, delighted to discover that her nipples were as sweet and responsive to his mouth as he had envisioned. And if he didn't linger over them quite as long as he had planned, it was only because of the urgency of her movements beneath him. He kissed his way across the soft swell of her stomach to the secret delights between her legs.

He groaned as her delicious essence flooded his senses, then settled in to explore. He was determined to find every place that pleased her, every place that made her sigh and quiver and come apart in his arms. But she was so delightfully responsive to his touch that the urgency swept over him once more and he sank into her body while she was still quivering from her most recent climax.

"That feels so good," she gasped, her body pulsing around him.

"Not too much?"

She clasped him so tightly it was difficult to believe that he was not causing her pain.

"No. More, Artek. Please."

His hips jerked forward, harder than he had intended, but another climax swept over her. Once again his careful control vanished in a wild rush of need. She met each stroke and when the overwhelming pleasure of his climax left him limp and gasping, she only pulled him closer. When he recovered enough to raise his head, she smiled up at him before her eyes fluttered closed.

"I think this was the best sweet moon ever," she whispered and fell asleep in his arms.

Sleep did not come as easily to him and he found himself staring into the dimly lit room.

Mated.

He still found it almost impossible to believe. He had grown up assuming that he would find a mate, but that had changed in the blink of an eye. He'd been about to set off for a visit to the capital for the winter season. A season of dances and concerts and introductions to females, one of whom he had hoped would be the right female to become his mate. When his father called him to his study, he'd only assumed it was about the upcoming trip.

Instead, he found the older male frowning down at his desk. Neither the frown nor the location was unusual. His father had many business interests and spent most of his time working. Artek had spent very little time with him or with his socialite mother.

"The Federation has attacked Vizal," his father said.

The planets in their sector were aligned into two coalitions. Kember was a member of the Galactic Alliance, while the others formed the United Federation. Vizal was a minor planet claimed by the Alliance.

"What does that mean?" he asked, already dreading the answer.

"It means we go to war." His father finally looked up, his face hard. "You will report to military headquarters to be assigned to a combat unit."

"But..."

"It is your duty. All oldest sons of fighting age are expected to serve, and you must lead the way. I will speak to you again before you leave," his father added, turning back to his data screen.

It was a clear dismissal, and he returned to his quarters in a state of shock. His valet was there, packing the wardrobe of clothes he had intended to take to the capital.

"Leave that, please," he said. "I would like to be alone."

The male gave him a surprised look, but didn't argue. As soon as he left, Artek went to the window overlooking his family's vast estates. Everything looked peaceful and prosperous in the morning sun, and the thought of war seemed almost unbelievable. His thoughts chased each other in ragged circles, unable to settle on anything concrete, until there was a quiet knock on the door and Callum entered.

"I heard."

Callum was his father's chief of security and the one who had begun Artek's own training. He had spent far more time with him than he ever had with his father.

"I don't want to go," he blurted out, expecting to see disgust on the other male's face.

Instead, Callum only nodded. "We can look for an alternative, although I understand they are already beginning to check any passengers leaving the planet."

Callum's calm acceptance of his reluctance helped steady him, and he gave the other male a rueful smile.

"It doesn't matter. I may not want to go, but I have no choice. It is my duty."

He wandered over to one of the open trunks and ran his fingers over the expensive silk of a formal shirt. "I suppose I won't need any of this now."

"No," Callum agreed. "We will need to pack lightly."

"We?"

"Of course. You didn't think I was going to let you go by yourself, did you? I will accompany you."

And he had.

Callum had been at his side through ten years of hell. Ten years of loss and pain and senseless destruction as they fought over what often seemed to be the same patch of land. In the end, it made no difference. The two governments had declared Vizal neutral territory, and both of them had abandoned the war-ravaged planet. Once again, his life had changed in an instant.

His father had died while he was serving, and his mother had found a new mate. He had no desire to return to Kember and a way of life that now seemed distant and unsatisfying. None of his males, his brothers, had anywhere to go. Endark had heard about the ranch from someone on Cresca, and Artek's inheritance had been large enough to fund the purchase. And so they had all ended up here.

Now he had a home and a mate, but that long-ago morning had taught him how easily his hopes for the future could be snatched away from him. Perhaps even the female sleeping so contentedly in his arms would be taken—or might choose to go. His arms tightened automatically, and she murmured a faint protest in her sleep. He forced himself to relax.

He did not deserve her, but he would make her happy. He would not fail her as he had failed so many others.

CHAPTER 8

Nelly looked ahead eagerly as they came over the final slope of the pass. As she did, she felt the slight betraying ache between her legs and couldn't help smiling. Last night had been a revelation. She'd had no idea that sex could be so completely, overwhelmingly enjoyable. Her experience with her suitor during their very brief engagement had not been unpleasant, but neither had it been particularly noteworthy. When she'd discovered his true colors and thrown him out of her life, she'd felt no need to seek out another man.

But Artek had shown her exactly what she'd been missing. The first time had been a little difficult, her body hovering on the edge of pain as he stretched her open, but then those marvelous ridges on his cock had stroked a place inside her that literally made her see stars. The very urgency of his desire added to her own arousal, reassuring her that he wanted her just as much as she wanted him. The second time had been a little slower but even more amazing as her body adjusted to him. And then this morning he had woken her with slow, drugging kisses, drawing out her anticipation before finally entering her and rocking her slowly into a sweet, unexpected climax. She'd still been gasping for breath when a knock sounded at the door.

"That will be Callum," he said with a regretful smile. "I wish we could remain here all day, but we must collect your belongings and get started in order to reach the ranch before night falls."

She nodded and he rose, still naked, and headed for the door. She was so busy admiring the powerful muscles of his back on the changing curve of his ass that it took her a moment to remember that she too was naked.

"Wait!"

She wrapped the sheet around herself, grabbed her clothes, and disappeared into the bathroom at the back of the office. Thank goodness Josiah's distaste for modern life had not extended to plumbing. Wainwright had an efficient modern system. By the time she emerged, trying not to blush, Artek had prepared her a plate of food from their neglected basket. He had insisted she eat before they went to face her father.

Their departure had gone better than she expected. Although her father was obviously unhappy, and kept scowling at Artek, he didn't make any attempt to persuade her to stay. She suspected that Miranda had convinced him that it was for the best.

Remembering their conversation the night before, she changed out of her dress into a pair of loose-fitting pants and a soft blouse. Her father gave her a scandalized look when she returned, but Artek smiled. The pants were far more practical for riding and really, it wasn't as if women didn't wear pants, although they tended to confine them to working around their homes. Her father had just insisted that she present a proper appearance in the store.

He had followed them out to the street, watching gloomily as Artek and Callum loaded her two small trunks on either side of one of the placid horse hybrids.

"You'll come back and visit," he said roughly.

"I will," she promised. "But not until spring."

He scowled, but didn't object, and she kissed his cheek before turning to Artek. He helped her into her coat, the brush of his fingers against her neck causing a reminiscent shiver. She expected him to help her onto the horse carrying her belongings, but instead he lifted her onto the saddle of his own horse and mounted behind her.

As they went down the main street, she could feel the eyes upon them, although after Artek's roar, almost everyone remained inside.

But Florie came out of her restaurant to wave at her, and Pearl was standing at her garden gate, Ruby next to her, her eyes wide with excitement.

"Have a wonderful winter," Pearl called. She smiled at Nelly, but she couldn't help noticing the way her friend's eyes flicked to Callum. That was interesting.

"We could come visit you," Ruby said. "It's really not that far."

Pearl sighed, and put her arm around her sister as if to stop her leaping over the fence. "We'll see you in the spring."

Once again, Pearl's eyes went to Callum before she blushed and looked down.

Nelly returned her goodbye, and then the town was behind them. The trail started climbing almost immediately, gently at first and then more steeply as they headed up the pass. They rode for several hours, and her body started to ache from the unaccustomed exercise, but she enjoyed the ride. Enjoyed the warmth of Artek's body behind her. Enjoyed the stunning beauty of the mountains, the peaks already capped with snow.

As they traveled, he told her a little more about the ranch and the types of stock they were raising. He and Callum talked briefly about some of the preparations they needed to make for the winter, but on the whole they rode in silence, accompanied only by the jingle of the horses' gear and the rush of the breeze.

Now that they had reached the top of the pass, she could see the ranch stretching down the valley in front of them. The area was wedged between the mountains, a wide swath of green with a river running along one side. Buffalo grazed in the pastures next to the river, a hybrid of the ancient Earth animal, ideally suited to the long, cold winters in the mountains, although he'd told her that they also raised hybrid beef cattle and hybrid sheep.

"That's the shed we use to store goods intended for sale," he said, pointing to a large wooden building to one side of the pass. "But most of the other buildings are down there."

She followed his gesture to a collection of buildings located about halfway down the valley on a slight rise overlooking the river. They were too far away to see many details, but she recognized barns and what looked like a stable, as well as the long lines of what must be the house. Her heart skipped a beat. Her new home.

"It's beautiful," she said sincerely. The trees covering the lower slopes had already donned their autumn finery, a hundred shades of red and gold mixed with the darker hues of the evergreens.

"We have made a lot of progress," Artek said as he urged the horse forward once more. "But there is still much work to be done."

Was that a warning in his voice? She smiled and put her arm over his where it rested around her waist.

"I'm not afraid of hard work," she told him.

But then they actually reached the house.

Callum took the horses and left Artek to show her around. The view from the distance had been misleading. Yes, it was large—and beautifully situated on a hill overlooking the river—but it was on the verge of being a complete wreck. The main central building was flanked by two long wings, both of which had sagging rooflines. So many shingles were missing from parts of the roof that she could actually see the exposed beams. Some of the siding had come off, and instead of what must once have been an attractive garden at the front of the house, weeds and vines threatened to obscure the entry.

Too appalled to speak, she followed him through the doors into the huge main room that occupied the center of the house. The windows that made up the entire far wall were thankfully still intact, as was the high vaulted ceiling. The view through the windows was stunning, but all she could see was the mess directly in front of her. Piles of crumpled bedding were strewn everywhere. Upturned boxes that were being used as tables were covered with dirty dishes and what looked like an engine was being disassembled in the middle of the floor. Other half-completed projects filled the rest of the space. It looked more like a workshop—an untidy workshop—than a home.

"Most of the bedrooms are down that hallway," Artek said, breaking the silence. "There are a few more on this side, including my—*our*—room, along with the kitchen, dining room, and office."

He headed down that hallway and she followed silently, praying that the kitchen was in better shape. It was not. More dishes covered the countertops, food-encrusted pots waited on the stove, and the floor seemed to cling to her feet as she walked over to the sink and turned the handle on the faucet. The pipes clanked and groaned, but only a few drops of brown liquid emerged.

"I assume you can cook?" Artek asked, his voice uncertain, and she whirled to face him.

"What?"

He shrugged uncomfortably, looking at the surrounding mess.

"I know the kitchen needs cleaning, but none of us have any skill at cooking. I was hoping you could teach us."

Teach him? It was all too clear what he actually wanted, and her chest ached.

"I thought you wanted a wife."

"I do," he said stiffly.

"No, you don't. You want a cook and a housekeeper. When you said this place needed a feminine touch, I thought you meant you wanted to make it more attractive and comfortable. I didn't realize you meant it needed rebuilding."

Before he could respond, Callum appeared in the wide archway leading into the kitchen, followed by more huge aliens. Her shocked gaze took in a feline male with deep rose colored fur and a giant green male with what looked like plant tendrils trailing down to his shoulders. Another male with coppery gold skin and wings—*wings?* —leaned against the arch, and a last male with silvery skin and a distinctly wolfish countenance scowled at her. *A Vultor?* She had never seen one before, but she heard them described often enough, usually accompanied by terrifying tales of savagery.

"Nelly, these are my brothers. Benjar, Gilmat, Drakkar, and Endark. Frantor isn't here."

"It's about time you got here." The feline male, Benjar, she thought, flashed her a grin that revealed disturbingly sharp fangs. "What's for dinner? I'm starved."

She saw Artek make a silencing motion, but it was too late. She turned on her heel and marched out, making it as far as the woods behind the house before she realized she couldn't see due to the tears streaming down her face. She hadn't realized until that moment just how much she had hoped this was going to be a real relationship. All those sweet touches, the way he had studied human customs—they hadn't been because he wanted to please her. They had been nothing more than a trap to lure her here.

What was it he had said last night? That he'd been trained to pleasure females? No doubt he'd been trained to manipulate them as well.

She stumbled over a half hidden root and came to a halt, clutching the trunk of the nearest tree.

Behind her she could hear yelling and what sounded like blows coming from the house, but she couldn't find it in herself to care. *What am I going to do now?* Go back to town and listen to her father lecture her? Face the curious, knowing glances of the other townspeople?

Or stay here, slaving away for seven aliens who were no doubt congratulating themselves on her foolishness?

Her knees trembled, threatening to give way, and she collapsed on a nearby rock, burying her face in her hands. Something fluttered past her face, startling her enough that she opened her eyes and saw a blue silk handkerchief had landed on her lap.

"Don't cry."

The voice was harsh, with an almost mechanical timbre, and she jumped, but when she turned her head there was no one in sight. Then she caught a flicker of movement behind a thick patch of undergrowth and remembered Artek had mentioned another brother.

"Frantor?" she asked cautiously.

There was no answer. She deliberately turned her back on the bushes before picking up the handkerchief and using it to wipe her face.

"Thank you," she said softly. "Won't you come out?"

"No."

"You might as well. Apparently, it's now my job to look after all of you," she added bitterly.

Another silence, long enough that she wondered if he was still there.

"It's not your job," he said finally. "You are Artek's bride."

"Doesn't that make it my job? Isn't that why he married me?"

"No," the harsh voice said firmly. "He married you because he wanted you to be his bride."

A tiny spark of hope ignited in her heart, but she shook her head.

"He's never actually said that."

There was another pause. "He hides his feelings. He thinks he needs to appear strong in order to take care of us. Ask him for the truth."

"I'm sure he's too busy having a good laugh at my expense."

The house had fallen silent, and there was no sign of Artek.

"He would never do that. Trust him."

The bushes rustled and she couldn't help turning her head to look, but all she saw was a faint metallic gleam. When she turned back to the house, Artek was walking towards her.

CHAPTER 9

Artek stalked out of the house, anger still simmering in his veins. How like Benjar to immediately make everything worse. The younger male had a good heart, but he was far too impulsive. *And dangerous*, he thought, shaking the hand he had damaged by slamming it into Benjar's rock hard jaw. Of course Endark had immediately sprung to his friend's defense, the violence that seemed to hover so close to the surface these days erupting. While Gilmat tried to pull them apart, Drakkar simply stood on the sidelines making satirical comments. It hadn't been until Callum returned from the barn and waded into the fray that order had been restored.

"Why the hell did you do that?" Benjar growled, his hand on his jaw.

"Because she's my wife, you idiot. She's not your servant."

"You said she would cook for us," Endark snapped, his fangs still extended. "When you told us all the advantages of having a female around the place."

He sighed. "What I said was that perhaps she could help us learn how to cook." None of them excelled in that department. "I still hope she can, but it will be her choice, do you understand me? I want her to be happy here."

The words were difficult to say out loud, but the tension in the room diminished. Both Callum and Gilmat nodded, and even Benjar gave a reluctant shrug.

"I guess I can understand that." Benjar's usual cocky grin resurfaced. "I won't ask her to feed me again."

He briefly grasped the younger male's shoulder. "Thank you."

"If you want her to be happy here, then I suggest you go after her," Drakkar said, raising a sardonic eyebrow. "In my experience, a female who runs away expects to be followed."

"I suspect at least in this case, you're right. And while I do that, see what you can do to make this place more acceptable," he ordered as he headed for the door.

To his relief, he immediately spotted Nelly sitting on a rock at the edge of the woods. At least she hadn't gone any further. But how could he convince her that she had misunderstood his intentions?

She looked up at him as he approached, and he could see the traces of tears on her face as he dropped down on one knee in front of her.

"I'm sorry. I should have explained that the house needed repairs. When we first arrived on the ranch, it seemed more important to repair the other buildings first."

"I can understand that. What I can't understand is why didn't you tell me what I was walking into."

He took her hand in his and although she didn't pull away, her small fingers didn't return his clasp.

"I could tell you that it was because it had always seemed satisfactory to us, because I had grown used to it, but while both of those are true, they are not the entire truth. I didn't tell you because I was afraid that you would not accept my offer."

She was still watching him intently.

"Did it matter that much to you?"

"Oh, yes. You've occupied my thoughts since the moment I saw you," he admitted. "I want you here with me, Nelly. Not to cook or to clean, but just to be here with me. You can lie in bed all day if you prefer, just as long as you stay with me."

Her expression finally softened, but she shook her head and his heart threatened to skip a beat. Was she going to leave him after all?

"The only way I'd want to stay in bed all day is if you were with me," she whispered, and then she leaned forward and kissed him.

Relief mingled with desire as he returned his kiss, and he suddenly wished they were back in last night's cozy room with nothing to worry about except for each other. But he had duties to fulfill and he reluctantly ended the kiss. Thankfully, she was still smiling as they rose to return to the house. Something fluttered to the ground as they did and she bent down and picked up a blue silk handkerchief which he recognized.

"Frantor was here?"

"Yes and no. I never saw him, but he spoke to me." She smiled up at him. "He told me to listen to you, and to trust you."

"I don't understand how he could say such a thing." He still blamed himself for the other male's injuries.

"He obviously thinks very highly of you. I just wish he didn't feel as if he had to hide. Why does he do that?"

"He was very badly injured while we were on a mission. We did the best we could, but by the time he could receive medical assistance, there was too much damage. He is badly scarred."

"That doesn't mean he needs to hide," she said indignantly.

"I agree, but all we can do is give him time."

She sighed and tucked her hand in his arm. "I suppose you're right. And I suppose we better go back so I can see just how much work needs to be done."

But although she gasped again as they walked into the main room, he could tell this time it was a gasp of pleasure. The dishes had been taken to the kitchen, the bedding had been assembled as neatly as if it awaited inspection and the various projects had been arranged as neatly as possible along one wall. All five of his brothers stood in a straight line as if they too were awaiting inspection.

She took in the sight and then started to laugh, a low, infectious sound that won answering smiles from everyone, even Drakkar.

"All right. If you're going to cooperate, then I suppose I can see what I can do about making dinner."

Benjar stepped forward, and bowed with a sweeping flourish.

"I apologize if I offended you."

"Maybe it wasn't the best time for you to make the suggestion."

"I'll work on the timing," he promised, then grinned, once more his irrepressible self. "I'll even volunteer to help wash the dishes."

"Now that's an offer I can't refuse. Let's get to work."

While he was happy to see her smiling again, he saw no reason for her smiles to be directed solely at Benjar and he tugged her closer against his side.

"I will assist as well." He could see the smile looking in her eyes, but she thanked him solemnly.

"I, on the other hand, have no intention of washing dishes," Drakkar announced. "But I will bring in firewood," he added when Artek glared at him.

The others also volunteered to perform various chores, and he smiled as he followed his female to the kitchen. Perhaps this was going to work out after all.

As Nelly returned to the kitchen, she hoped that her initial impression had been wrong and that it wasn't really as bad as it had seemed at first glance. She had not been wrong. If anything, it was even worse on second look.

She sighed and tried to concentrate on the positive aspects. The room itself was a good size with a row of windows over the sink looking out the wooded slopes of the mountain behind the ranch house. A door on the same wall opened out onto a covered porch with a rustic table and chairs. Beneath the stacks of dishes was a wide wooden countertop and well-built lower cabinets. There was a pleasant room somewhere beneath the mess.

"I know the pipes don't work, but I assume you get water from somewhere?" she asked Artek.

He nodded. "There's a pump house to pull water from the river. It is just not connected to the plumbing for the house right now."

"I'll fetch some water," Benjar volunteered.

He grinned at her and disappeared with a flick of his tail. *A tail.* She shook her head. And she'd thought Artek and Callum were different when they first showed up at the store.

"What can I—*we*—do to help you?" Artek asked.

"Let's start by making space in the sink. I think some of these dishes are going to need to soak, especially without any hot water."

"That, I can remedy," Drakkar said as he entered with a load of firewood. He looked around the kitchen and shook his head. "Barbarians."

"You contributed," Endark growled, glaring at him.

"I would never allow my lair to deteriorate like this."

"You mean you don't live here?" she asked.

"It's... complicated."

"He thinks he's too good for us," Endark said derisively.

A brief flash of something that might have been hurt crossed Drakkar's face.

"You know that's not true," he said quietly, then bent over and started loading some of the wood he had brought into the stove.

He did something she couldn't see and the wood burst into flames. After he removed the dirty pots from the top of the stove, he nodded at her.

"I suspect you will need more wood. I will return shortly."

He headed for the doorway, but as he did, Endark reached out and briefly touched his arm in what was clearly an apologetic gesture. Drakkar gave him an equally brief nod, but she saw his shoulders relax as he went on his way. The bonds between these males were obvious and she suddenly understood why Artek had called them his brothers. They reminded her of the Mickelsons—one of the local farming families. Five strapping brothers who seemed to argue constantly, but woe betide anyone who tried to take on one of the brothers. The other four were immediately at his back.

Benjar returned with two large metal buckets full of water, and she told him to put them on the stove and fetch more. He agreed willingly enough, and she set to work.

Half an hour later, the kitchen was finally in reasonable shape. Some stubborn dishes were still soaking and the floor desperately needed mopping, but the counters and table had been cleared and wiped down. It was time to think about a meal.

As if in response to her thoughts, Gilmat appeared at the kitchen door with a box overflowing with vegetables. He had tried to help in the kitchen as well, but he was so big that she kept bumping into him. His size intimidated her at first, but his shy smile and hasty apologies had quickly won her over. When Benjar made a joke about his greenhouse, she sent him off to gather vegetables. The box he handed her now was full of some of the best-looking produce she'd ever seen—huge, healthy potatoes and carrots and onions.

"This is the best I could do," he said shyly as he handed them over.

"These look wonderful," she told him.

A shadow seemed to cross his face, but he nodded. "They'll do."

They would more than do, but since the subject seemed to bother him, she didn't pursue it.

"I have cleared the table as you requested."

Callum appeared at the entrance to the kitchen. The wide archway that opened into the kitchen was mirrored by a corresponding arch on the other side of the hallway that led into an enormous dining room. The huge table had also been covered with junk, most of it so old and dusty that she suspected it had been there since Josiah's time, and she'd asked him to clear it off.

She followed him back to the dining room, noticing that it too had a vaulted ceiling and a wall of windows overlooking the river. Now that the table was clear, she could see that it had been formed from one huge wooden slab, the beautiful grain gleaming in the late afternoon sunlight. He'd even polished the table.

"It's very sad, isn't it?" she said to Artek as he joined them.

"What is, sweetness?"

The endearment seemed to slip out unintentionally, and her heart fluttered, but she did her best to keep her face calm as she gestured at the room.

"I was just thinking about Josiah. He designed this huge table—this huge house—and he must have expected to fill it with his family. Instead, he ended up living here all alone. No family, no friends. At the end, only one of his servants remained."

"Yes, Baylor. We met him," Callum said. "He remained on the ranch until we came. We offered to let him stay, either in the house or one of the other buildings, but he said he was tired and wanted to go home."

She had met Baylor several times over the years when he came to town on a rare shopping expedition. He was an elderly man with a kind smile and a dignified air.

"Where did he go?"

"He didn't say, but he didn't seem unhappy to leave."

Artek hesitated, then put his arm around her, and she leaned against his big, warm body.

"The house is no longer empty. We are already a family. I hope we will fill it with more family, just as Josiah intended."

She smiled up at him, her heart filled with warmth at the promise of his words, but nodded at the kitchen.

"We better start by feeding the family we already have."

When they returned to the kitchen, she frowned thoughtfully at the box of vegetables as she tried to decide what to cook.

"Where do you keep your food supplies?" she asked.

He opened a door on the far side of the kitchen to reveal an enormous pantry, the shelves stocked with supplies, many of which she recognized as coming from her father's store. *Enough for an entire winter,* she thought. It was a reminder that she would soon be confined on the ranch until spring, but despite the challenging beginning, the knowledge didn't trouble her.

"There is also cold storage on the lower floor," he added.

"I'll take a look at it tomorrow, but for tonight this will be fine. Do you think soup will be all right?"

"Anything they do not have to try and cook will be perfect," he assured her.

She laughed, and set to work.

CHAPTER 10

*A*rtek sat at the kitchen table, chopping vegetables as Nelly had requested. She had chased the rest of his brothers out of the kitchen, but hadn't objected when he told her he would stay and help. Although he wasn't helping as much as he could since he was paying more attention to her than his task.

She moved easily around the kitchen with those quick, graceful steps of hers, humming beneath her breath. *It's almost as if she's dancing,* he thought. Now that she was his, he could watch her as much as he wanted. He no longer had to try and disguise his interest. And now he knew what lay beneath her clothing—the smooth skin and delightful breasts, the delicious sweetness between those strong thighs.

Once again, he wished that they were alone, that he could pull off her clothing and stretch her out across the table as his own succulent feast. His cock jerked at the image, and he almost cut himself.

"Watch what you're doing," she scolded him. "I don't think having part of your finger in the soup is going to add to the flavor."

"No, I'm not as delicious as you are."

Her face was already flushed from the heat of the stove, but he saw the color deepen on her cheeks.

"Really?"

"Yes," he said firmly, and then surprised himself by reaching out an arm and pulling her down onto his lap. They were alone in the kitchen, but he could hear his brothers in the living area and any one of them could walk into the kitchen. He didn't care. Having her in his arms was more important than maintaining his usual controlled image.

She didn't protest, smiling up at him. She had pulled her hair back in its familiar tight braid that morning, but between the ride and the work it had loosened, and dark tendrils curled softly around her face. He stroked one of the silky strands between his fingers.

"I could feast on you for hours," he murmured.

He caught the sweet scent of her arousal, even as she shook her head.

"I think we'd better feed your brothers first. But maybe later..." she added shyly.

"Definitely later."

He couldn't resist kissing her, and immediately lost himself in the sweetness of her mouth. She responded just as enthusiastically, and he was on the edge of lifting her to the table when a crash from the next room reminded him that they were not alone.

"What was that?" she asked, eyes widening.

Her lips were red and swollen from his kisses, inviting more, and he had to force himself to respond to her question instead of kissing her again.

"If I had to guess, I would say Benjar. He leaves a trail of chaos in his wake."

"Was he with you the entire time you were... fighting?"

"No, he was one of the last to join us." So many males had passed under his command, males he had been unable to save no matter how hard he tried. "It was about three years before the end."

"Maybe that's why he doesn't seem as much like a soldier as the rest of you."

He gave her a rueful smile. "Don't let his appearance fool you. He has never responded well to military discipline, but he is a deadly fighter and courageous enough for two other males."

"What about the others?" she asked curiously.

"Callum has been with me since the beginning, from before the war. Frantor was also part of my first squad. He lived on the planet where we were fighting. As did Drakkar," he added. "He came down from his mountain to join us perhaps a year later. And then Endark and Gilmat came together, about halfway through the war."

"Endark and Gilmat? They seem like a strange combination."

"They have more in common than you would suspect," he said, but didn't elaborate on his statement. Their stories were not his to share. "And they were not exactly volunteers. The war was not going well at that point, and the Alliance was... encouraging anyone they encountered to join the military."

Forcing was more accurate, but he still hated the idea that the side for which he had fought had been so ruthless. But the other side had been just as bad, and he had long ago stopped believing that either side was right.

"Did you volunteer?" Her eyes had darkened sympathetically as she listened.

"It was my duty," he said shortly, hoping that she wouldn't ask any more questions.

Perhaps she recognized his reticence, because she brushed a much-too-short kiss across his mouth and rose to her feet.

"I'm guessing they would rather I was feeding them than talking about them, so I'd better get back to work. And you too. Those vegetables won't chop themselves."

"Yes, sweetness."

Once again, the endearment slipped out without conscious thought, but she only gave him a brief pleased smile before bending back over her pots.

They sat down to dinner just as the sun was setting, the last rays illuminating the colors of the autumn foliage in a blaze of glory, and he saw Drakkar give a long glance out the window. The other male struggled with extended periods surrounded by others, but Artek was grateful that he had joined them—that they were all together for this meal. It felt appropriate to welcome Nelly into their home this way.

"I suppose you don't have electricity either?" she asked as Drakkar lit the candles.

"We do, but we've been using the generator to power the workshops. I'll see what we can do about restoring power to the house."

She looked around the candlelit dining room and smiled at him.

"I don't think there's any hurry. This is nice." As she returned to the kitchen to fetch another plate, she bent over and whispered in his ear. "After last night, I'm very fond of candlelight."

Endark barked out a laugh as she left. "You should tell your little bride that several of us have very sensitive hearing."

More pleased than embarrassed, he simply grinned at the other male. "Which is why our room is at the far end of this wing."

The others laughed, but now that he had mentioned their room, he couldn't help wondering about the condition of the bedroom. They had all chosen rooms in the house when they first arrived, but between the decrepit state of the roof and long habit, they all usually ended up sleeping together in the living area. He hadn't actually slept in the room in a long time, and he'd only given it a perfunctory inspection before leaving for town.

Nelly returned just in time to see Benjar reaching for the bread she had made, and she promptly smacked his hand. His youngest brother yelped and gave her a startled look.

"What was that for?"

"Because we don't eat until everyone is at the table. Didn't anyone teach you manners?"

"No," Benjar said cheerfully. "Do females care about manners?"

"Yes," Drakkar said, raising an eyebrow. "You cannot expect to find a bride of your own unless you can behave in a civilized fashion."

"I don't need manners. I'll simply impress her with the size of my—" Benjar yelped again. This time, Artek had been the one to smack him. "And what was that for?"

"There will be no discussion about your... parts in front of my bride."

"You're just jealous," Benjar muttered, and Nelly glared at him.

"I can assure you, he has no reason to be jealous."

A stunned silence fell before everyone burst into laughter. Pleased by his bride's defense, he grinned at his brothers and squeezed her hand under the table.

The laughter set everyone at ease, and conversation flowed freely as they started their meal. He hid a smile as he realized that both Benjar and Endark were paying attention to the way she placed her napkin across her lap and gracefully used her utensils. Drakkar's manners were always impeccable, as were Gilmat's. Both Artek and Callum had been trained on how to behave during a meal, but he suspected that neither Endark nor Benjar had ever had such instruction.

Nelly's food was a huge success, and they devoured every mouthful. She gave them a pleased smile and promised to cook more the following day. Remembering her earlier concerns, he shook his head.

"It is not fair for you to do all the cooking. We can take it in turns as we did before."

There was a collective groan from the rest of the table, and she laughed and shook her head.

"I really don't mind cooking, especially since I also enjoy eating and it doesn't sound as though any of you are capable of producing something edible. As long as you're all willing to help with cleaning up and fetching water and those types of chores, I'm willing to keep cooking."

Heartfelt vows of assistance immediately followed her words, and Benjar jumped up to start clearing the table. As the rest of his brothers followed, Artek pulled Callum to one side.

"Keep an eye on everything and make sure everyone behaves. I'm going to check on our room."

"Of course, but I don't think you need to worry. Your new bride seems quite capable of keeping them in line. You did the right thing to bring her here," his second added.

"I hope so. I want her to be happy."

"It is your job to make sure that she is. So go and make sure that she has an appropriate place to rest."

CHAPTER 11

Nelly smiled as she looked around the now clean kitchen. The males had been as good as their word, but despite that, exhaustion suddenly swept over her. It had been a long, tiring day, and thanks to Artek she hadn't had much sleep the night before. And what had happened to him? He'd disappeared after dinner, and even though she'd had plenty of help, she found herself looking for him. Maybe she should ask Callum where he had gone.

But then two big warm arms slid around her from behind and a familiar scent filled her head. She put her hands over his and leaned back into his embrace.

"Tired, sweetness?"

"Just a little. Maybe we should have an early night."

"Mmm." He leaned down and nibbled at the curve of her ear, sending a surprisingly erotic shiver of pleasure through her body.

"I meant to sleep," she said, laughing, but it wasn't really a protest. His obvious desire for her both comforted her and aroused her own desire.

"Then sleep you will," he promised as he picked her up in his arms and headed down the hallway.

As he stepped around a patch of leaves that had blown in through a hole in the roof, she did her best not to sigh. Hopefully the room he was taking her to was at least weathertight.

Double doors waited at the end of the corridor, and he carried her through them before putting her down.

"This is wonderful," she said, looking around with a sigh of relief. A large bed with an ornately carved wooden frame stood on one side of the room. On the other side, glass doors let out to a balcony with a panoramic view of the river valley. There were some signs of damage—a cloth had been tacked up over what she suspected was a broken window, and there was another heap of leaves brushed into a neat pile in the corner—but the room was basically intact.

The bed was the only furniture in the room, but it had been neatly made and covered with a thick blanket. Another one of the big stone fireplaces was on the far wall, the fire already lit to ward off the evening chill. When she moved around the bed towards it, she saw the bath. A copper bathtub with a high curved back, steam rising gently from the water, waited in front of the fireplace.

"I thought the plumbing wasn't working."

"It's not, but I thought you might appreciate a bath to soothe your aches." He could have been referring to the strain from the long ride, but from the heat in his eyes, she suspected he was referring to an entirely different kind of ache. "I brought in the water and heated it, and I will do so every night until the plumbing is restored."

It was such an unexpectedly thoughtful gesture that her eyes filled with tears.

"Thank you. It means a lot to me that you did this."

"I want you to be happy here. I do not have any experience with pleasing a wife, so you will need to let me know if there is anything you require."

"You do very well with pleasing your bride."

She pressed her fingers lightly over his cock before heading for the bath. He followed her every movement as she started to unbutton her blouse, and she remembered his fingers skating across her skin when he had performed the same action the previous night. Her nipples tightened at the memory. She was tempted to ask him to help her, but she suspected if she did, she might not make it into the bath and she really didn't want to waste his gift.

That didn't stop her from keeping her movements slow and sensuous as she finished unbuttoning the blouse and slipped out of her pants before removing her under things. The air in the room was still cool, but between the warmth of the fire and the heat in his gaze, she wasn't the slightest bit cold. Her nipples were tight little peaks, but it wasn't due to the temperature.

She stepped into the tub and sank down into the hot water, sighing with pleasure as it surrounded her, immediately beginning to soothe her aching muscles.

"This feels so good," she murmured, resting her head against the tall back.

He didn't respond, and when she looked over at him, he was still standing at the entrance to the room.

"Would you prefer to be alone?" he asked stiffly. "I understand that humans prefer privacy for their bodily functions."

"Not this human—at least not when it comes to bathing," she added hastily. "I'd rather you stay and keep me company."

He muttered something she couldn't hear, but came and sat down next to the tub.

"What did you say?" she asked.

"I was reminding myself that I needed to give you time to enjoy your bath first."

"First?"

"I believe you offered me another treat. Later."

The heavy ache between her thighs was back, and she was almost tempted to abandon the bath. Almost.

"I'll make it a short one," she promised, and he smiled at her.

Silence descended over the room except for the pop and crackle of the fire and the distant rush of the river. Even though they weren't talking, she was supremely conscious of the fact that he was there - that she was not alone. Contentment settled over her like a warm blanket—contentment mixed with the teasing promise of what was to come. Perhaps it was time to move things in that direction.

When she opened her eyes, he was still watching her. His eyes were golden with arousal, but his face was relaxed, more at peace that she remembered ever seeing him before.

"If the plumbing isn't working, where have you been bathing?"

"In the river."

She gave an exaggerated shiver, and he smiled at her.

"It is somewhat cold," he admitted. "And even if it were warmer, you must promise not to try bathing there. The current moves too swiftly for your small frame."

"I'm not really that small." As a matter of fact, most of the men in town found her too tall. They preferred small, curvy females like Pearl and Ruby.

"You are small to me," he said firmly, and she couldn't argue.

"I don't suppose you have any soap?"

"I do, but I was so entranced by your beauty that I forgot."

For someone who could be so stiff, he could also say the sweetest things.

He went through the door next to the fireplace and returned a moment later with a bar of soap. It was one of the ones they sold, but it was so expensive she'd never actually used it. She unwrapped it eagerly, enchanted by the delicate floral fragrance.

"I love the way this smells."

"Your own fragrance is far more delightful."

Her heart melted a little more, and then she had an idea. A wonderfully wicked idea.

"If you bathe in the river, then you know how to use this, right?"

"Of course."

He looked mildly insulted, and she hid a smile.

"In that case, can you help me wash my hair?"

He almost tripped over his feet as he stepped towards her. She loved his eagerness.

She unfastened her braid, and ducked beneath the water. Once her hair was wet, he began working the soap into the long strands, his strong fingers massaging her scalp and infinitely gentle as he slowly, thoroughly washed her hair. She rinsed her hair, and then stood up in the tub.

"And now the rest?"

He obeyed, washing her body as slowly and thoroughly as he had washed her hair. His big hands slid across her breasts, pulling briefly on her aching nipples before moving on. He lifted one leg, even washing between her toes before sliding his hands up over her calves and upper thighs, hovering at the edge of her sex before moving to the other leg. He washed her back and arms before finally moving to the patch of curls between her legs and rubbing the soap across her needy flesh.

"You are so beautiful here. So small and pink and perfect." His finger hovered at her entrance. "So small it seems impossible that you can take me."

She heard a note of doubt in his voice and put her hand on his shoulder.

"I think last night—and this morning—proved quite successfully that I can take you."

"You are a miracle. I never thought I could deserve—"

He stopped speaking, the shuttered expression returning to his face for a moment, and she squeezed the firm muscles beneath her hand.

"You're my miracle too." Her throat unexpectedly tight, she tried to lighten her voice. "Are you through bathing me?"

"Not quite."

His soapy fingers traveled up and down her folds, and even delved between her buttocks. She shuddered when he tapped lightly at her back entrance, and he gave her a thoughtful look, but then he resumed the slow strokes, circling her now swollen clit but never actually touching it.

Arousal sang in her veins, and she tightened her grip on his shoulder, trying to urge him on, but instead he smiled.

"And now I will rinse you."

He poured water over her, carefully checking to make sure that no trace of soap remained before he wrapped the towel that had been waiting by the fire around her and lifted her free. Instead of putting her down, he carried her to the big bed.

"But I'm still wet," she protested halfheartedly.

"And you will soon be wetter," he promised, and he was right.

He covered her freshly bathed body with kisses then settled between her legs and eagerly licked up every trace of her arousal before attending to her long neglected clit. As soon as his mouth closed over the swollen bud, she climaxed, her body quivering as long waves of pleasure rippled through her.

Instead of rising over her as she expected, he only smiled and started all over again. He drew out his explorations even longer this time and when she finally climaxed a second time, it washed over her so powerfully that when she finally stopped shaking, her whole body was limp and exhausted. As her eyes drifted closed, she felt him running a damp cloth gently over her body before pulling her into his arms.

CHAPTER 12

*E*ven though Artek's cock ached with unsatisfied need, he smiled as Nelly settled in his arms. He looked around his room—*their* room—with an appreciation he hadn't felt before. He had originally chosen it simply because it had been the furthest from the rest of the house. Like Drakkar, he sometimes needed to get away from his duties and the reminder of his failures. He still didn't think he deserved the female resting so trustingly in his arms, but she had chosen him, however unlikely that seemed, and he would not let her down.

Forcing his mind to more practical matters, he started a mental list of things that needed to be done to ensure her comfort. Fortunately, the bedroom itself had not been in terrible shape except for one broken window. The bathroom on the other side of the fireplace was another matter. Part of the roof was missing and needed to be tended to as quickly as possible. He had no intention of sending his bride to the latrine they had built in the trees any longer than necessary.

He was still adding to the list when he finally fell asleep.

The next morning he woke her with kisses, and this time she did not fall asleep after he pleasured her but reached for him instead. He was still smiling when he entered the kitchen. Drakkar had already lit the stove and provided more firewood. Benjar gave him a cheerful grin as he placed two buckets of water on the stove.

"Morning, Commander. You look very... rested."

"I slept very well, thank you," he said calmly as he went into the pantry.

"As did I," Nelly added as she joined them.

She smiled at him, and Benjar groaned.

"Are you two going to be like this every morning?"

"That is my intention."

"You are a god among men," she told him sincerely when he handed her the bag of coffee he'd retrieved from the pantry. He found the substance distasteful, but he knew that many humans enjoyed it.

"A god?" Benjar sniggered as he reached past Artek to grab a piece of the bacon Nelly was laying out. When Artek smacked his hand, he growled at him. "Would you stop doing that?"

"No, he won't, because he's a god," Nelly said, smiling up at him. "And he remembers what I said last night about manners."

"Even in the morning?" Benjar looked appalled, and she laughed.

"All the time."

Benjar snatched another piece of bacon before Artek could stop him, and Nelly frowned.

"You do know that's raw, right?"

Benjar shrugged. "It's meat, is it not?"

She gave his fangs a horrified look, then turned back to the stove.

"In this house, we cook the meat."

Benjar gave him a puzzled look behind her back, but he only smiled. None of them were particularly worried about eating raw meat, with the possible exception of Gilmat. During their combat years, they had eaten whatever they could find, but he had no intention of telling Nelly about that time.

Everyone reappeared for breakfast, except for Frantor. He sighed as he looked at the empty chair and decided he would go and check on the other male later that day.

"I'm going to work on the roof this morning," he announced, looking around. "What are your plans?"

"I'm going to do some blasting," Endark said. He was moodily eating the now cooked bacon and ignoring Nelly's delicious pancakes. "I want to divert the stream that flooded the high pasture last spring before winter sets in."

Artek suspected the other male also wished to go for a run in the woods, but he only nodded.

"I'll be in the greenhouse. Callum said that the new strain of fruit stock isn't developing as well as we had hoped." Gilmat's face was as calm as usual, but Artek knew him well enough to see the worry in his eyes. Gilmat was capable of achieving amazing things with plants, but it never seemed to satisfy him.

"Before you go any further," Nelly said, taking a sip of her coffee. "I've been thinking about what you said last night. All of you offered to take turns at cooking—"

"We didn't offer—the commander volunteered us." Benjar grinned at her.

"Being volunteered is part of military life," Drakkar said sardonically.

Nelly ignored them both. "As I said last night, I'm willing to continue cooking. Where I do need help is with the rest of the house."

"What's wrong with it?" Endark asked, his tone edging on belligerent. He definitely needed a run.

"It's falling apart. The roof is falling in, the siding is coming off, and all—or at least most—of the interior is filthy. I intend to start by scrubbing the kitchen floor, but I could use some assistance."

"There is still work to be done on the ranch," Drakkar said, not argumentatively but simply stating a fact.

"I know that. What I was thinking is that each of you could take it in turns to assist me. Maybe one each day?"

She gave him an inquiring look, and he almost responded that he was the only one she needed to help her, but he stopped himself in time. It would be good for all of them to participate in this aspect of the ranch. It was easy to focus on the work and not on building a new home. He hoped that assisting her would help cement that feeling. And it wouldn't hurt any of them to be exposed to her civilizing influence.

"Do we get extra food if we help you?" Benjar asked.

She laughed. "No, but if whoever's helping me that day does a good job, I'll make a treat for after dinner."

"Then I volunteer for today," Benjar said, his tail lashing eagerly.

Once again, he bit back the urge to protest. Of all of his brothers, Benjar would benefit most from Nelly's influence—although he would drop a word in the other male's ear to remind him to behave.

After they finished their meal, he somewhat reluctantly left them to clean the kitchen while he went to work on the bathroom roof. He was perched on the ridge pole placing shingles when Drakkar flew up to join him, carrying more shingles, and he gave him a surprised look. The other male usually preferred chores that he could perform by himself.

"I can manage here if there are other things you need to do."

Drakkar shrugged, his wing fluttering, before he settled down next to him.

"It is far more efficient for me to bring you the shingles than for you to make multiple trips up and down that ladder, earth dweller."

Despite his sardonic tone, Drakkar smiled as he looked out across the valley. "You chose well."

"We were lucky that Endark had heard it was available."

They worked in silence for a few moments, before Drakkar spoke again.

"Your bride seems... content."

"I hope so. I intend to do everything in my power to make sure that she is happy." He gave the other male an inquiring look. "Do you not long for a bride—a mate?"

"It is not the custom amongst my people."

Drakkar very rarely spoke about his people. All Artek really knew about them was that they occupied the high mountains of Vizal and that they had disapproved of Drakkar joining the military. Most of them had remained aloof from the fighting until the last terrible years. He kept silent, hoping that the other male would continue.

"You know that we do not do well in constant contact with others. That extends to our own meetings. We come together briefly, and then part. What social gatherings we attend are always outside under the sky. Matings are arranged at those gatherings."

"Did you ever attend one?" he asked.

"I intended to, but the female in whom I was interested was killed during the first year of fighting." His wing fluttered again. "That is when I decided to join your band."

"I'm glad you did," he said sincerely.

"There were many times when I wished I had not," Drakkar said dryly, then looked around the valley once more. "This is not one of those times."

Drakkar bent over and picked up the hammer, his confidences at an end.

As Artek also returned to work, he caught a flash of silvery green entering the pumphouse. Frantor must be working on something. He was by far the most obviously scarred of the brothers, but none of them had escaped the war undamaged, he reflected as he watched Drakkar frowning down at his work.

But then he looked up at the mountains soaring into the crystal blue of the sky and smiled. If there was anywhere they could find peace, this was the place.

CHAPTER 13

"What would you like me to do first, Commander?" Benjar asked Nelly as soon as the others left.

"Just Nelly will be fine."

"Whatever you say, just Nelly," he said with a grin, and she rolled her eyes.

She supposed she should be afraid of him. He was easily a foot taller than her, and in addition to those wicked fangs, he had equally vicious claws tipping each finger. But despite those threats, he reminded her of Ferdie. Big and cheerful and well meaning, although occasionally thoughtless.

"We're going to start by scrubbing the kitchen floor. A floor should not stick to one's feet."

"I bet I could walk across it without sticking."

There was a hint of challenge in his eyes, and she had the sudden suspicion that he was not quite the friendly kitty he was pretending to be, but she ignored the provocative look.

"I can't, and I intend to be able to walk across it without sticking. It makes me a better cook," she added, and he grinned, the challenge gone.

"In that case, where do we begin?"

"By getting everything off the floor. Can you help me move the table?"

"I don't need your assistance for that, just Nelly."

He picked up the sturdy wooden table without the slightest hint of strain, and she did her best not to look impressed.

"Can you put it in the hallway? We can stack chairs and anything else that's on the floor on top of it, then move it back in here once the floor is clean and we're ready to start on the other floors."

"Others?" he asked and gave an exaggerated sigh. "Why did I volunteer to be first?"

"Because I lured you with my cooking."

"I am a slave to my appetites," he agreed, and gave her another challenging look. "All of them."

"The only one I'm interested in is your desire for food. Now are you going to work, or stand there talking all day?"

He gave her what looked like a respectful glance and grinned.

"Just checking. I don't think the commander has a lot of experience with females."

"And you have?" she asked as she filled a bucket with soapy water.

"At one time I had a female in every port."

"That sounds exhausting," she said dryly as she handed him the first bucket and started on a second bucket for herself.

"Well, perhaps not in every port." His expression sobered as he picked up the mop. "But none that mattered. I envy the commander."

The last was said so quietly she almost didn't hear him.

"It's certainly not too late. You're not exactly over the hill."

He gave her a confused look. "No, I'm right here."

"I meant you're not that old."

"Perhaps not physically, but I am not the man I used to be." Once again, his mercurial temperament changed, and he gave her a cheesy grin. "So you will have to teach me everything there is to know about human females."

"I'm not sure that I'm an expert. We're all different, just as all of you are different."

"Can you at least tell me what females like?"

"Well, I enjoy cleanliness," she said with a pointed look, and he dutifully resumed his mopping. "I also like baths. And candles," she added with a reminiscent smile.

"I see. Do all females enjoy those?"

"Maybe not all of them, but I think most of them do. My friend Florie enjoys cooking."

"Don't you?"

She shrugged. "I think it's more accurate to say that I don't mind cooking, and I do enjoy eating. Florie has a real gift."

"Baths, candles, and food." He nodded. "Got it."

She laughed. "As I said, it varies from woman to woman. My friend Julie enjoys flowers and books. Ruby likes pretty clothes. I'm not really sure what Pearl likes. I'm not even sure that *she* does."

"Why not?"

"Because she's been too busy looking after other people, especially her sister, to think about herself."

"I see." He hesitated. "The commander is like that. But now I think he knows what he likes."

His grin was friendly rather than insinuating, and she smiled at him before concentrating on the floor.

It took three changes of water and a last scouring on their hands and knees before the wide painted boards of the kitchen were clean enough to suit her.

"Excellent," she said with satisfaction. "Now we can move on to the dining room."

Benjar groaned, but didn't protest as they switched locations. They worked together for the rest of the day and he continued to pepper her with questions about human females. He didn't shy away from more intimate questions, but took her refusal to answer them in good part.

He even helped her to prepare dinner, and he was the one who gave an outraged yell when Endark started to track mud into the kitchen.

"I spent all fucking day cleaning this floor, you animal."

Endark snarled and lunged at him, and a moment later the two of them were rolling around on the kitchen floor, snapping and growling. Her temper snapped. She grabbed the broom and started whacking any available body part.

"Stop that this minute or I'm going to send both of you to bed without any supper."

Two startled faces looked up at her, so shocked that her anger disappeared in a burst of laughter.

"Dammit, I worked for that supper," Benjar protested.

"I worked," Endark growled, but despite his obvious hostility, she thought she saw a trace of vulnerability in his eyes. "I deserve to eat."

"Of course you do. I was just trying to get your attention. I have every intention of feeding you both. But I do expect you to wipe your boots before you come into the house," she added.

He hesitated, still looking oddly uncertain despite his fearsome appearance.

"Go on," she urged him. "I made cookies for dessert, and I still have some left, despite Benjar's attempt to eat them all."

"Cookies?"

Benjar grinned and patted his stomach.

"They are excellent. Come on. I'll help you get rid of the mud."

Endark jerked a nod, and the two males disappeared.

After supper, Artek and Callum cleaned the kitchen while Drakkar started a fire in the huge living room fireplace. All of them gathered around it, and when Artek joined them, she leaned back in his arms, listening contentedly as they swapped stories.

"It's your turn, Nelly," Benjar said at last.

"I don't really know any stories," she protested.

"Nothing from your past?"

"I haven't exactly had an exciting life."

"Then what of your people?" Callum suggested. "Perhaps a historical incident?"

She thought back over the history she had learned, an odd combination of ancient earth history and what she suspected were somewhat apocryphal tales of the town's founding—a product of Josiah's ideas as to suitable education. There was one story she remembered very well—it had been one of her favorites when she was a romantic schoolgirl, and she thought it might appeal to them given their history.

"Once upon a time, there was a group of Roman soldiers coming home from war."

"Roman?" Gilmat asked.

"Rome was the capital city of a mighty empire, and its soldiers were famous for their strength and bravery."

The big male nodded and sat back.

"The soldiers were looking forward to settling down and starting their families, but they returned to their lands to find that all of the women had gone. The war had lasted so long that they had all left to find new homes."

There was an exchange of looks, and she suddenly wondered if the story was getting a little too close to home. She hurried on.

"They didn't know what to do, so they consulted the local wise man—a man who had lived in the nearby hills for as long as anyone could remember. And he told them what to do."

"What did he tell them?" Benjar asked eagerly.

"He said that there were plenty of women in the town across the river. He said that soon there would be a celebration and the women would be dancing and full of joy. He told them to go there and find their wives and then bring them home."

"Just like that?" Endark asked skeptically.

"Well, not quite as easily as that. Of course the men in the other village protested when the soldiers tried to carry their brides away, but the soldiers threw them over their shoulders and carried them off into the night."

She'd always thought that part was so romantic. And even if Artek hadn't exactly thrown her over her shoulder and carried her off, their whirlwind courtship felt the same.

"Did the men of the other village go after them?"

"Of course they did. But the Romans were strong and brave. They carried their women over the river and through the woods and deep into their own country, arriving just as winter was about to begin." She smiled at Artek. "The Romans settled down with their wives, but the men of the other village did not give up. When spring came, those men arrived in a mighty force."

"And the soldiers fought for their brides," Endark growled.

"They didn't have to. Their brides told the men of the other village to go away. They said that they were happy with their soldiers. So the men left and they all lived happily ever after."

"An interesting tale," Drakkar said thoughtfully.

She laughed as she rose to her feet. "I always enjoyed reading it when I was in school. Now, who is going to bring in water for the morning?"

To her surprise, none of them stood. Instead, Artek smiled at her.

"There's no need."

"What do you mean there's no need? I'll need the water for coffee and washing dishes and—"

"Try the tap," he urged her as he guided her into the kitchen. All of the brothers followed them.

She turned the handle, just as she had done the previous day, and this time, there was a faint gurgle and then clear water gushed down into the sink.

"It works! That's wonderful. Who fixed it?"

"Frantor did," Endark said. "He's the mechanic."

"But he doesn't even come to the house."

There was an exchange of glances.

"He's not far away," Endark said finally.

"I wish he would come and join us," she sighed.

She hesitated, then picked up a plate and piled it with the few remaining cookies before walking out onto the porch. Endark had said that Frantor wasn't far, and she thought he'd meant it literally. She stood there for a moment, looking into the darkness, and something gleamed in the deep shadows beneath the trees. A flash of light reflecting off metal?

"Thank you for fixing the plumbing, Frantor," she called into the night. "You are always welcome here, but if you don't want to come inside, these are for you."

She placed the plate on the small table and went back inside.

In the morning, the plate was gone.

CHAPTER 14

Two weeks later, Nelly walked out of the front door and smiled at the transformation. She had struggled with finding a task that suited Gilmat. He moved gracefully, especially for a male of his size, but he always seemed slightly awkward and uncomfortable inside. Remembering his skill with vegetables, she had finally come up with the idea of asking him to work on the garden area around the front entrance. The results were almost miraculous.

The weeds had been cleared away, replaced by an astonishing variety of small, healthy bushes. The overgrown vines surrounding the door had been trimmed back and were actually blooming, despite the lateness of the season and the increasingly frosty nights.

The rest of the repairs were coming along just as successfully. Drakkar and Artek had focused on the roof whenever they had time, and most of the shingles had already been replaced. Since Endark also preferred to work outside, he had been steadily repairing the damaged siding. She still couldn't decide exactly what to make of the Vultor male. His temper flared so easily that he was constantly fighting with the rest of his brothers, but despite that vein of anger she could see underlying hints of loneliness and uncertainty.

She tried getting him to talk about himself, but he was extremely reluctant. All she knew for sure was that he had been born here on Cresca. When she'd asked him if he had family here, he gave her a smile that was equal parts bitter and lonely.

"I have no family—except for my brothers."

She decided not to press the matter and changed the subject. Despite his reluctance to talk, he seemed fascinated by Wainwright and listened eagerly to anything she had to say about the town.

To her surprise, Benjar had turned out to be her most reliable assistant. Being inside didn't bother him, and most days he helped her for at least a little while as she did her best to restore cleanliness and order to the house. The next time he was helping her, she asked him about what Endark had said about his lack of family.

He shook his head. "Endark's original family rejected him because his father was not Vultor."

"That's terrible," she said indignantly.

"I agree, but there are many who do not approve of breeding outside their species. How do humans feel about it?"

She started to spring to the defense of her species, but then remembered that first town meeting. "I hate to admit it, but I'm sure there are those who would disapprove."

"Will that stop you?" he asked curiously.

"Stop me?"

"From having a child with the commander?"

"Oh, no."

She could hear the longing in her voice. Artek seemed convinced that they could have a child together, but she couldn't help wondering if they were too different. If it didn't happen, she had already decided to talk to him about adopting. Given the band of brothers he had already acquired, she didn't think he would object.

"That's good," Benjar said thoughtfully, and she gave him a suspicious look. Whenever he got that distant look on his face, she had learned that it generally meant he was coming up with some outrageous scheme.

"Why is it good?" she demanded.

"Because I can't wait to be an uncle. I'm sure I will be an excellent one."

She laughed, even though she suspected that there had been more to his question, and asked him to pull down the tattered curtains. He had accepted the change of topic, but she was thinking about babies again when Callum walked up to the house.

"I believe it is my day to assist you," he said, and she gave the older male a warm smile.

He was so reserved as to be almost taciturn, but his affection for Artek was quite clear, and she had rapidly come to appreciate his steadying presence amongst the other more volatile brothers.

"I think you're the only one who remembers the schedule," she told him as they returned to the house.

"Do you need me to remind them?"

"It's not necessary. Once they understood what I wanted them to do, they started working on those projects whenever they got the chance."

"I have noticed," he agreed. "But you haven't assigned me any ongoing projects."

"Mainly because I know how busy you are. But there is something you could help me with today."

"Of course," he said courteously, and followed her past the dining room to the room that Artek used as his office.

"I'd like to tidy up in here, but I don't want to disturb anything important. Can you help me pick those out?"

"I would be happy to assist you." He gave her a penetrating look. "Why is this important to you?"

"I think Artek will appreciate it. Even though he never complains, I've noticed that he's more relaxed when things are neat and orderly."

"His father was very insistent on orderliness and I suspect that influence still lingers," he said as they started going through the items on the cluttered desk.

"What was his father like?"

"Busy. Too busy to spend much time with Artek, and the time they did spend together usually involved his father pointing out the areas where he needed to improve."

She sighed. "My father can be like that too, but he's never ignored me and I know he loves me." She'd missed him more than she expected, but she was still convinced that she had chosen the right path.

"What about Artek's mother?" she asked.

"She was very... social. She preferred to remain in the capital. He saw very little of her either."

"Is that why—"

When she didn't continue, Callum gave her an inquiring look.

"Is that why he's so reluctant to let me help him?" she blurted out, her frustration overcoming her discretion.

It seemed silly to complain about the fact that he was so thoughtful to her, but it was beginning to feel uncomfortably one-sided. Even when she could tell he was worried about something, he never wanted to discuss it with her. Their lovemaking, as wonderful as it was, was always focused on her pleasure rather than his.

Callum considered the matter as he filed a set of papers he had removed from the desk.

"I believe it is a factor. He never had a chance to witness a true partnership between a male and a female. It also did not help that he was put in charge of a squad at such a young age. He took the responsibility very seriously and never asked anyone to share his burdens."

"I wish he would share them with me."

"You'll have to show him the way. I do not think it will be easy, but he cares very much about you," he added softly.

"I... care about him too."

I love him, she thought silently, but she wasn't about to admit it to Callum before she told Artek. And she had not yet found the courage to tell him. Neither had he said anything to her. She believed that he cared for her, but for now, she kept her feelings to herself.

Neither of them spoke as they finished clearing the desk. She polished the surface and then Callum returned the items he had marked as important. The two of them worked in companionable silence as they cleaned the rest of the room and she smiled with satisfaction when they finished. She could hardly wait until Artek saw it.

She took him there after dinner, but his initial look of pleasure almost immediately changed to a frown.

"You did not need to do this, sweetness."

"I know I didn't need to, but I wanted to. Don't you like it?"

"Very much." He smiled as he ran his finger over the polished wood of the big desk. "I should have attended to it long ago."

"You were busy," she said softly. "And I was happy to do it. Now come with me."

He looked as if he were about to protest again, but instead he took her hand and followed her down the hallway to the bedroom.

"Take off your clothes and lie on the bed," she told him.

He didn't hesitate to obey, but he gave her a curious look. "Why?"

"Because tonight I'm going to focus on pleasing you," she whispered as she slowly removed her clothes.

His eyes followed her with their usual hunger, and he was hard and ready when she joined him on the bed. Unfortunately, the rest of the evening didn't go as planned. She had barely started kissing her way down his body when he flipped her over and started kissing her instead. Her protests disappeared in the rush of arousal he created so easily, but even though he left her as limp and satisfied as always, her frustration reappeared as she stared into the darkness.

The next morning, she awoke before him and decided to try again. He could hardly take over while he was sleeping. She cautiously wiggled her way down his body, doing her best not to disturb him, until she reached his cock. He was already half-erect, and she gently traced the marvelous ridges covering his shaft. His cock responded instantly, hardening beneath her touch, but from the sound of his breathing he was still asleep.

She put her hand around him then started licking her way gently up his shaft, tracing the swirling ridges with her tongue. He moved restlessly beneath her, but when she glanced up at him, his eyes were still closed. It wasn't until she closed her mouth around the broad head, that he jerked awake.

"Nelly! What are you—"

His question ended in a groan as she sucked him deeper into her mouth. Drops of pre-cum danced across her tongue, as sweet and salty as she remembered from that first night.

He made another attempt to protest, but she ignored it as well, using her hand to work the lower part of his shaft since she couldn't take all of him in her mouth. His hand hovered over her head, and for a moment she was afraid that he would attempt to pull her away. Instead, he whispered her name in a hoarse voice, then buried his fingers in her hair and urged her on. She gladly complied, taking him as deeply as she could and moving faster as she felt him swell even more beneath her hand and mouth, his hips rising to meet her until he finally exploded in a rush of salty sweetness.

Her body hummed with arousal, but she ignored it as she pressed a final kiss to his shaft. Satisfaction filled her as he pulled her up into his arms.

CHAPTER 15

"Why did you do that?" Artek asked as soon as his racing pulse steadied.

She gave him a happy smile, her eyes heavy with satisfaction. "Because I wanted to. Didn't you enjoy it?"

"I do not have the words to convey how much I enjoyed it, but it is my duty to pleasure you."

"Duty?"

Some of the pleasure drained from her face, and he saw the green sparks appear in her eyes.

"Perhaps that is not the right word," he said quickly. "It is my honor."

She gave him a thoughtful look, but somewhat to his surprise, she didn't comment further. Instead, she rose and began dressing for the day.

"Why are you leaving? I have not yet pleasured you."

"I already told you that I enjoyed touching you so don't worry. Your duty is done."

She stalked out of the bedroom with a distinctly icy expression on her face.

He was still worrying about it when he rode out with Callum to check the fences later that morning. Nelly's mood had softened over breakfast, but he couldn't help feeling that he had done something wrong.

"Your female is concerned about you," Callum said, breaking the silence in which they were riding.

"Concerned about me? Why? Am I not doing something correctly?"

Callum sighed and brought his horse to a halt.

"It's been almost two years since the war ended. You do not have to be in control all the time."

"But it's my responsibility."

"No, Artek. This ranch is a joint responsibility. We all chose to come here, and we all chose to work. There is nothing wrong with sharing that responsibility." Callum gave him a grave look. "Your female also wants to share that responsibility."

"I do not want her to worry. I want her to be happy."

"She will be happier if you talk to her. If you share your concerns with her."

"Do you really think so?"

"I do. A true partnership involves supporting each other. It can't all come from one side."

Without waiting for a response, Callum set his horse in motion again, leaving Artek to ponder his words as he followed. Was his second correct? A few nights ago, she had been asking him about the ranch accounts, and he had kissed her instead of responding. He had thought that focusing on her pleasure would be more satisfying for her, but now he remembered the frustration on her face before she had returned his kiss. Perhaps Callum was right.

He was still considering the matter when they reached the tree line. He sighed and turned his attention to another one of his duties.

"You go ahead. I want to check on Endark."

The other male had not joined them for meals for the past two days and although Artek knew that he was healthy, the isolation worried him. Callum nodded, and Artek headed along the tree line.

There was a stone shepherd's hut located at the upper edge of the pasture, and Endark had claimed it as his own. He often spent the night there since it provided access both to his flock and the woods if he wished to run.

No smoke was coming from the chimney, and Artek frowned as he dismounted and headed for the door. There was no immediate answer when he knocked.

"Endark? Are you in there?" More silence answered him, and he was about to return to his horse, when the door was flung open and Endark glared at him.

"What do you want?"

"I was worried about you."

And with good reason, he thought. The other male was disheveled, his hair thick and wild, and his fangs very apparent.

"There is no need to worry," Endark lied and started to close the door, but Artek held it open and followed him inside. The place was a wreck. Torn bedding was scattered in pieces across the floor, and he could see long scratches on the inside of the door.

"What have you been doing?" he asked. "Why haven't you come to the house?"

Endark prowled restlessly around the room before stopping in front of the window, his head bowed.

"I have been trying to practice control, but I am failing."

"What are you trying to control?"

"The need to change, to run. How can I expect a human bride to understand that? And I need a bride. My people do not function well without a mate."

"I think perhaps you are underestimating the human females," he said at last. "I believe that a true mate would understand your needs."

He realized he was echoing Callum's earlier words and shook his head. Why was it so much clearer when it was someone else?

"Do you really think so?"

The hope on Endark's face was almost painful to see.

"I do. The right female will understand your need to run. Although you may find that once you find her, the need subsides."

He joined Endark at the window, grasping the other male's shoulder as they looked down on the peaceful valley.

"This is a new start for all of us, and I believe it can be a good one."

"Perhaps you're right."

"I certainly hope so. Now stop fighting your instincts and go for a run. If it would make you feel better to have a purpose, Callum said he saw adyani tracks at the edge of the upper meadow."

The native predators tended to keep to the upper slopes of the mountains, but he didn't want them harassing their herds over the winter.

Endark grinned, his fangs flashing.

"I'll take care of it," he promised.

"Good. And come to dinner. Nelly worries about you."

Endark's face actually softened. "You have a very caring mate. I hope that I will be as lucky."

"I'm sure you will."

He gripped Endark's shoulder again and left. He'd barely mounted his horse when he saw a flash of grey emerge from the hut and he smiled. It appeared that Endark had taken his advice after all.

Since he was already this high on the ridge, he decided to continue along the ridge line and check on Benjar. His youngest brother was using all of his spare time to renovate one of the line cabins—although he was far too enthusiastic about Nelly's cooking to ever miss a meal.

The last time Artek had seen the cabin it had been almost derelict, but as he approached it now, the rotting planks had been replaced by clean new wood and the roof was freshly shingled.

Benjar must have heard him coming, because the sound of hammering inside the cabin stopped and he came out to greet Artek.

"Greetings, Commander. What are you doing up here?"

"Just admiring your handiwork. You've done a lot of work since the last time I was here."

"I am preparing a den for my bride."

"You could also bring her to the main house," he offered. "All of you have been working so hard that most of the rooms are habitable now."

"No, thank you," Benjar said firmly, and Artek did his best not to smile at the polite reply. Benjar had obviously been paying attention to Nelly's lectures on manners. "I want her all to myself, at least at first."

He couldn't argue with that. There were still times when he wished that he and Nelly were alone.

A shadow passed over them, and they both looked up to see Drakkar soaring higher up the mountain.

"Do you think he's also preparing his lair for a mate?" Benjar asked.

"I did not get the impression that he intended to seek a bride."

"Perhaps it's just as well. What female would want to live in a cave in the mountains?"

"I suspect you're right. Are you joining us for dinner tonight?"

"Of course. Nelly is making a roast." Benjar grinned at him. "I checked with her this morning."

Artek laughed and rode on, already eager to return to his bride.

To his relief, she no longer seemed to be annoyed with him, and the rest of the day proceeded like any normal day. He had just finished helping her clean the kitchen when she came back in from the porch, frowning down at a plate of cookies.

"What's wrong?"

"I don't know, but Frantor didn't come and get his cookies last night. You said he lives in the workshop further down the river, right? Maybe I should go and check on him."

"I don't think that would be a good idea," he said gently. "He prefers to keep to himself."

"But what if he's hurt? How would we even know?"

"I would know."

"How?"

He hesitated, then led her into the office and handed her his datapad. She gave the screen a puzzled look.

"What is this?"

"A topographical map of the valley. This is the river, and this is where we are."

"I see. But how does having a map help?"

He pressed a button and seven small lights appeared on the screen, each one a different color. One of them was at their location.

"This is me," he said, tapping the small blue light.

"I don't understand."

"All soldiers were implanted with a tracking chip, so we knew where to find them if they... could not make it home."

Her teeth closed over her lower lip, and he knew she understood the implications of his words.

"We discussed taking them out when we arrived here, but we decided not to do it. I think we find it comforting to know that we are connected this way—to know that none of us will ever be lost."

She put her arms around his waist and hugged him. He let himself take comfort in her embrace before he cleared his throat and pointed at the map again.

"This pale green light—that's Frantor. He's in his workshop. He spends most of his time there, although I've noticed that he's making regular evening trips to the house."

"Because of the cookies?"

"I suspect so. Perhaps they will eventually lure him inside."

"I could make a trail of them leading to the door," she suggested, and he smiled.

"I don't believe he would fall for that, but then again, I never expected him to make it this far."

"Thank you for showing me," she told him quietly. "I like it when you let me know what's going on."

He could hear the echo of Callum's warning in his head, and he nodded.

"Callum has been reminding me that I tend to keep things to myself. I was trying to make life easier for you, but I think perhaps it was having the opposite effect."

"I want to be part of your life, Artek. All of it, not just the good things. I want this to be a partnership between us."

"I want that too, and I will do my best to remember that you will be happier if I tell you what's happening," he said, and then smiled. "And if you wish to pleasure me again as you did this morning, I will not object."

She laughed and took his hand.

"So was it Callum's wise words or my efforts this morning that helped you understand?"

"Perhaps both."

When they entered the bedroom, moonlight flooded the room. She crossed to the glass doors and opened them onto the small balcony. A cold breeze swept into the room, a hint of snow in the air, and he went to join her, folding his arms around her as she looked up at the sky.

"Look at the moons," she whispered.

Both moons hung low and full in the sky, shedding a silvery light over the entire valley.

"The larger moon is almost full. Almost time for the harvest dance."

There was a wistful note in her voice, and he hugged her closer.

"Do you wish to attend?"

To his relief, she shook her head. "I don't think so. Not this year. I hope that by the spring, everyone will have gotten used to the idea of us being married. And my guess is that Miranda and Pa will get married as well once he realizes I'm not coming back."

She turned around in his arms and smiled up at him. "So no dance this year."

"We can have our own dance."

He took her hand and whirled her back into the bedroom, and she laughed with delight.

"You know how to dance?"

"I was taught." His father had not approved, but he considered it a necessary part of his education.

"If they taught you as well as they taught you other things," she said with a teasing smile. "Then I expect you're an expert."

"Judge for yourself."

He whirled her around the bedroom under the light of the moon before taking her to bed for an entirely different dance.

CHAPTER 16

A week later, Nelly prowled around the kitchen, feeling unusually restless. She'd been feeling tired for the past few days, and Artek had insisted that she remain in bed that morning.

"I worry about you," he added, and she sighed and agreed.

She could tell that he was making an effort to be more open about his concerns, and the least she could do was listen to him. He was also trying to be more receptive when she wanted to take care of him, although she could tell he struggled with it.

She'd actually enjoyed the extra sleep, but now the house fell curiously empty. Snow had fallen on the upper slopes overnight, and all of the brothers had gone to check on the herds and move some of the animals down from the upper pastures. It was the first time she'd been left completely alone, and she hadn't realized until this moment how much she had grown used to having company.

Don't be silly, she scolded herself. *They're working, and I should do the same.* They were sure to be cold and hungry when they returned. She prepared a big pot of stew and set it on the back of the stove to simmer.

Once that was done, she wandered aimlessly through the house, noticing all of the improvements. The big living room was no longer a chaotic mess of half completed projects. There was an equally large room on the lower floor and it now served as a workshop when they wanted to work on something inside the house. The sturdy log furniture that had been in the room originally had been returned, and she was working on recovering the tattered cushions. Most of the bedrooms in the far wing were now habitable and all of them had claimed a room, although they rarely slept there. But perhaps they would tonight after a long, cold day.

I should do something special for them, she thought, and decided to make some pies. With any luck, there would be enough late berries to fill them. She pulled on her outdoor boots and wrapped her cloak around her shoulders before stepping outside, but she still shivered when the wind swept past her. Grey clouds loomed heavily overhead, obscuring the tops of the mountains. Definitely a day to spend indoors. As soon as she had picked the berries and made her pies, she would build a fire and work on her cushion covers next to the fire.

There were still a few ripe berries on the bushes by the river, and she set to work gathering them. It might not be quite enough, but she could always supplement them with some dried fruit. She was just stripping off the last few when she heard a low growl from behind her.

Her heart leapt to her throat as she whirled around. An adyani stood only a few feet away, its teeth bared in a fearsome snarl.

She'd heard stories of the vicious predators, but she'd never seen one before. Thick, shaggy fur disguised an agile body, the hooves on each foot suited to the high mountains where it normally lived. They were supposed to keep to the upper ranges, but this one didn't seem to have received the message. She took a cautious step backwards, and it matched her step. Damn. She had no hope of outrunning it. Maybe she could scare it off...

"Go away!" she yelled as loud as she could, but it only growled again.

Oh, God, what was she going to do? She took another step back, and once again it matched her, but it still didn't come any closer. If it continued to keep its distance, maybe she could make it back to the house.

She took a firm grip on her basket. It wasn't much of a weapon, but it was the only thing she had to defend herself with. Once again she took a step back, and once again it followed her. Her heart was thudding against her ribs so hard that she felt sick, but she kept going. Step back, pause. Step back, pause.

It continued to mirror her movements, but its strides were longer than hers and the distance between them was shrinking. She tried to take a longer step, but she missed her footing and fell backwards, slamming her head against a rock as she hit the ground. The world spun around her in dizzying circles as the adyani growled again. She tried to remain conscious, to hold onto her basket and defend herself, but darkness kept washing over her vision.

Another growl sounded from behind her. *Two of them?* she thought dizzily, but then she caught a flash of pale green skin as someone—or something—passed her. More growls and the sound of fighting and then a yelp, abruptly cut off.

A face appeared over her, swimming in and out of her blurred vision. Scars and metal and oddly metallic-looking skin, but the eyes were human and worried. They were the last thing she saw before she lost consciousness.

When she awoke, she was back in her bed. Had she been dreaming? But the ache in her head was all too real—it couldn't have been a dream. But how had she gotten back here? She started to raise her hand to her head, and hot fingers closed around her hand and pulled it back down.

"I have just bandaged your wound. Leave it alone."

She recognized Drakkar's sardonic voice and turned her head to see him standing next to the bed.

"What happened?"

"You were attacked by an adyani. Frantor killed it and brought you back here."

There was a flicker of movement over by the window, and she thought she saw someone disappear onto the balcony. Drakkar sighed.

"And he's gone again."

"Frantor saved me?"

"Apparently, he heard you yelling at the adyani. A foolish gesture, but it alerted him to the fact that you were in trouble. He brought you back here and summoned me."

"How?" Her head was still pounding and her thoughts moved sluggishly.

"Because no one can reach my lair, Artek instructed me to keep a communicator on hand." He hesitated. "I saw him when I was coming here so I don't imagine it will be long before he arrives."

"I hope not."

She didn't think she would feel safe again until she was in his arms.

"Does he know?" Drakkar continued, and she gave him a confused look.

"Know what?"

Drakkar raised an eyebrow. "That you are pregnant, of course."

The room spun around her again, from shock this time.

"I am?"

"I detected it as soon as I examined you. You truly did not know?"

She started to shake her head and then thought better of it.

"It can take a while before a woman knows. Six weeks or more."

"How primitive." He tilted his head, listening to something she couldn't hear.

"It seems that Artek has arrived."

And then Artek was there, carefully lifting her into his arms as she burst into tears.

CHAPTER 17

"I think I am growing soft," Artek told Callum as they finished herding the last of the animals down from the upper pasture.

"Why do you say that?"

"Because I do not enjoy being cold and wet. I would rather be at home with my bride."

One of Callum's rare smiles brightened his face.

"I don't call that soft. I call that sensible. Why don't you return to the house and I'll finish up here?"

He shook his head. "It's my—"

"Responsibility. Yes, I know. But perhaps for once you should forget about responsibility and think about your bride. She is all alone."

Before he could respond, there was a flash of gold overhead and they looked up to see Drakkar winging his way past them.

"Artek," he called. "Your female... injured."

The words trailed behind him as he flew towards the house, and the breath seemed to freeze in Artek's lungs.

"Did he say... injured?"

"He did. Go," Callum ordered. "I'll close the gate and be right behind you."

He was already on his way, riding harder than he had ever done before, his fear an agonizing knot in his chest. He couldn't lose her. The refrain beat through his head over and over as he raced towards the house. He rode straight up to the door and flung himself off the horse, racing inside.

Nelly was in their bed, her face pale and a bandage circling her head, but her eyes focused on him immediately. With a prayer of thanksgiving, he gathered her into his arms as she began to sob. He did his best to comfort her as he gave Drakkar a frantic look.

"What happened?"

"She was almost attacked by an adyani, but Frantor got there in time."

"Thank the gods. Where is he?"

Drakkar shrugged. "You know how he is. As soon as he knew she would be all right, he left."

Remorse seared through him. He had failed again.

"I never should have left her."

Despite her tears, Nelly must have heard him, because she hiccupped a protest.

"Don't be silly. It wasn't your fault."

"A sensible statement, as always," Drakkar said, picking up his medical kit and heading for the door.

"Wait a minute." He gently lowered Nelly back to the pillow and hurried after his brother. "Why are you leaving?"

"Because there is nothing else to do. I cauterized the wound and bandaged her head. She'll be fine."

"That's it? How do I tend to the wound? Should she remain in bed? For how long?"

Drakkar sighed. "I told you. She's going to be fine. She's a sensible female—let her decide what she is capable of doing."

There was an underlying note of warning in his voice that made Artek frown, but he was too anxious to return to his female to pursue the matter.

"And you'll keep the communicator on?"

"Of course." Drakkar shook his head. "Now stop questioning me and go back to Nelly."

He willingly obeyed.

As soon as he returned to her side, her eyes fluttered open and she smiled at him. "I'm glad you're back."

"I never should have left you. It's all my fault." The weight of his failure crashed down over him. Once more he had failed.

"Would you stop that? It's not your fault. If it's anyone's fault, it's mine. I just never thought that there'd be anything dangerous down by the river."

"You were by the river?"

A whole new set of horrible possibilities appeared in his mind. What if she had fallen in? If she had been swept away? He shuddered.

"I should have taken better care of you."

"It's not your fault," she said again. "Why do you always blame yourself?"

"Because it would not be the first time I failed someone I cared about."

An expression flashed across her face too quickly for him to read.

"A female?"

He shook his head. "No, a close friend. Barat and I went through training together and he was also appointed to command a squad. It was the first year of fighting on Vizal, and it was… chaotic."

It had been a disaster. The Alliance were trying to build an army from soldiers gathered from many different systems. Aside from all the difficulties that entailed, the administrative functions were even more chaotic. Supplies of everything from food to weapons were misallocated or not replenished.

Three months after the fighting began, he received an urgent message from his friend. They were running out of ammunition and facing a much larger enemy force. He had gone to Barat's assistance, but by the time he arrived, it was too late. Barat and his entire squad had been killed.

"I was too late, just as I would have been too late this time."

"And it wouldn't have been your fault, just as it wasn't your fault before." He expected to see disgust on her face, but instead her eyes were warm as she smiled up at him.

"I am so afraid of failing you. I love you, Nelly." The words emerged with a rush of relief. He had been holding onto them for so long. "I can't stand the thought of losing you."

Once again, something flashed across her face that he couldn't read.

"What did Drakkar tell you?"

"Not to fuss over you. To let you decide what you are capable of doing."

"And that's all?"

His heart skipped a beat. "Is there something more? Have you suffered other injuries and he was afraid to tell me?"

"It's just my head, at least as far as injuries go. That's really all he said?"

"Yes, why?"

"I just wondered why you told me you love me."

"I should have told you a long time ago, but I didn't want you to feel obligated to return the feeling."

She shook her head, but the warmth had returned to her face.

"And you thought that keeping a distance between us would be better? The next time you decide to say, or not say something, please talk to me first, okay?"

"I promise."

"Good. Because I love you too."

Happiness rushed through him so quickly he felt dizzy. "Really?"

"Really. And it's just as well," she added thoughtfully.

"Why is that?"

"Because we're going to have a baby."

The world swayed around him once more, this time taking him to his knees next to the bed.

"I could have lost you both."

"But you didn't. I'm here—we're here—and everything is going to be all right. Now come here and hold me. I'm feeling sleepy, and I want to fall asleep in your arms."

He obeyed immediately, his heart singing with joy. A wife and a child. The future he had hoped for was finally coming true.

CHAPTER 18

At Artek's insistence Nelly remained in bed the next day, but by the afternoon of the following day, she was tired of her room. Outside the windows, a gentle snow was falling, turning the valley white, and she wondered if she could convince her family to take a snow day.

"And I'm pregnant, not an invalid," she muttered as she climbed out of bed.

Carefully removing the bandage from around her head, she was glad to see only a small pink mark remained from her injury. Drakkar had done an amazing job of healing the wound. She pulled on a simple dress and went to find her husband.

He and Callum were sitting at the kitchen table drinking coffee and she smiled. Both of them claimed to dislike the beverage, but she had noticed them drinking it with increasing frequency. Artek rose to his feet as soon as he saw her.

"I was just about to check on you. Are you sure you should be out of bed, sweetness?"

"Yes," she said firmly.

She could tell that he wanted to argue, but instead he only pulled out a chair for her.

"We were discussing what to prepare for dinner," Callum said solemnly, but she saw the smile in his eyes and gave an exaggerated shudder.

The food they had prepared over the past few days had not been particularly successful. At least they had kept the kitchen clean.

"Where's Benjar? He's watched me enough not to oversalt the soup or burn the toast."

They both winced.

"I did warn you that none of us could cook," Artek said ruefully.

"After you lured me here."

A shadow crossed his expression, but before she could reassure him, he smiled at her.

"I would have done whatever it took to have you marry me."

She returned the smile, then looked around the empty kitchen.

"Is everyone still working? I thought maybe we could have a snow day."

Callum raised a brow. "A snow day?"

"You know—sit around the fire and drink hot chocolate and tell stories."

"That sounds most pleasant, but it will only be the three of us. Gilmat is watching over a new planting, and you know Frantor won't join us."

She sighed. Artek had gone to see the other male, both to thank him and to ask him to come and see her but he'd refused. As soon as the snow stopped falling, she had every intention of marching down to his workshop and telling him herself, even if all she could do was to yell her gratitude through the door.

"What about Drakkar? Or Benjar and Endark?"

"They're not here," Artek said.

"Why not?"

"I told them about the harvest dance, and they decided to attend."

"Really?" She gave him a doubtful look. "Are you sure that's a good idea? The townspeople weren't even used to seeing you and Callum, and you've been coming to Wainwright for two summers now. Those three are going to be a shock."

He shrugged, but Callum looked up from his mug.

"They may not actually attend the dance. But in the words of wisdom you gave us, you said to seek their wives while they would be dancing and full of joy."

"Words of wisdom?"

"Yes." Callum frowned at her. "Do you not remember? You said the soldiers went to seek their wives at a dance and carried them off. Benjar and Endark intend to do the same, although Drakkar only went with them because he thought it would be entertaining."

"What?" Her mouth dropped open. "You don't mean they're just going to take women without asking?"

"Those were the words of wisdom."

"Would you stop saying that?" She turned to Artek. "You knew about this?"

"I knew that they intended to seek their brides."

"By kidnapping them?"

"As you described in the history you recounted."

She closed her eyes, praying for patience.

"That was just a story—it wasn't intended as a guideline. Oh my God, those poor women. They'll be so scared."

"They do not need to be afraid," he said, giving her a puzzled frown. "You know my brothers will not hurt them."

"But they don't know that! And what about their families? They're going to be worried sick. How would you feel if someone came along and stole one of your brothers?"

Artek and Callum exchanged a look.

"Perhaps this mission was not well planned," Callum said finally.

"You think? Please tell me it's not too late to call it off."

Both males looked out the window at the softly falling snow.

"The pass will still be open. I'll go after them." Callum rose to his feet, but shook his head when Artek started to rise as well.

"There is no need for you to come. You should stay here with your wife and child to be."

"But it's my—" Artek stopped, and turned to look at her. "What do you want me to do, Nelly? Accompany Callum and attempt to remedy this situation? Or remain with you?"

She bit her lip. Even though she was still upset by the fact that he'd known what was going to happen, she could believe that it had been a misunderstanding. She didn't want to be here alone, and she had no doubt that Callum could handle the more impetuous brothers.

"I want you to stay," she said softly. "Are you sure you'll be all right, Callum?" she added, looking out at the snow.

"Of course."

He nodded at both of them and left.

"Do you think he'll be in time?"

Artek hesitated. "I don't know. They left this morning so they have a good start on him. It would depend on their actual plans?"

"You don't know?" She couldn't help the bitterness in her voice, and he looked at her solemnly.

"Although I knew of the plan, I did not know the details. I should—" Once again, he stopped and shook his head. "Perhaps I should have inquired more closely, but I cannot control their actions."

"No," she agreed.

He sighed and reached for her hand. "It is difficult to let go."

"I know. And I know it was hard to stay here and let Callum go after them. Thank you for asking me."

"I only want you to be happy."

A lump appeared in her throat, but she managed a smile.

"Some unburnt toast would make me happy."

He laughed and, under her watchful eye, prepared an acceptable meal. They ate in the kitchen, but the cozy atmosphere only made the steadily increasing snow outside seem more threatening. She saw him sneaking a glance outside at least as often as she did, and she finally rose and took his hand.

"Let's go to bed. Sitting here worrying isn't going to change anything."

He nodded and followed her. Determined to distract both of them, she asked him to remove his clothes and lie on the bed as she had the previous time. This time when she kissed her way down his body, he remained in place, although she could see his fingers fisting in the sheets.

She teased his cock until it was rock hard and weeping, then climbed on top of him. Instead of lowering herself onto his cock, she rested her knees on either side of his hips and slid slowly along the thick shaft. Her folds opened around his shaft, those amazing ridges awakening every sensitive nerve.

"Nelly, I..."

"This is pleasing me," she assured him. "Isn't it pleasing you as well?"

"Gods, yes." His eyes glowed as he watched her move, the firelight dancing across her body, and his hands slid up to hover over her breasts. "May I?"

"You may," she said graciously, then gasped as he tugged firmly at her aching nipples.

She leaned into his hands, pressing her swollen clit against the ridged surface of his cock. Oh God. She rocked harder, letting her arousal build until her entire body was perched on the edge of climax, and then she looked down at him. He was holding himself rigid, his muscles straining as he forced himself to remain still.

"Now, Artek. Now take me."

He grabbed her hips before she even finished speaking, bringing her down over his cock in one powerful thrust. Her body exploded, her climax rushing over her in a tidal wave as he thrust up into her again and again, as fierce and wild and urgent as that very first night. All she could do was cling to him as wave after wave of pleasure rolled over her until he finally cried out her name and filled her with a rush of heat that triggered one last climax.

He pulled her down on top of him, holding her tight as she sighed with satisfaction.

"I am no longer sure who is pleasuring who," he said eventually, and she heard the smile in his voice.

"Good. That's the way it's supposed to be."

"My miracle," he whispered, and she smiled as she drifted off to sleep.

Sometime during the night, she thought she heard Artek roaring. She awoke with a start, but the room was dark and quiet so she snuggled closer to him and went back to sleep.

The next time she opened her eyes, the world outside the windows was a swirling cloud of white. The gentle snow had turned into a fierce blizzard. Artek was no longer beside her, and she hurried off to find him.

He was in his office, staring down at his datapad with an odd look on his face, and her heart skipped a beat.

"What is it? Is someone hurt?"

He slowly shook his head. "Everyone appears to be fine."

She went to join him, and he pulled her onto his lap. She breathed in his spicy scent and snuggled against him, her momentary panic fading.

"Why are you looking at the tracking screen? Did something happen?"

"There was an... avalanche last night. Or what seemed to be an avalanche."

"What do you mean by *seemed to be?*"

"Did I ever tell you that Endark is an expert with explosives?"

"I remember him talking about blasting," she said slowly.

"Yes. And look." He pointed to the screen. "Benjar and Endark are back in their dens. Drakkar is back on his mountain, although he's not responding to my calls."

"What about Callum?"

"He's here." He tapped on a purple light close to the edge of the pass. "That's the storage building we passed. He should be safe enough there until the storm passes."

"So everyone is back and safe?"

Relief swept over her and she smiled up at him, but instead of returning her smile, he kept staring at the screen.

"What is it?"

She could see him trying to decide what to say and was afraid he would just tell her not to worry. Instead he looked her directly in the eyes.

"I don't think it was a natural avalanche. I think they found their brides and brought them back here, then used an explosion to block the pass. That's why Callum is so close to it. He must have arrived around the same time."

"Oh no. We have to find out if they brought women back with them."

She started to climb out of his lap, but he kept his arms around her as he swung the chair around and pointed at the swirling cloud of white covering the window.

"We can't go anywhere until the storm passes."

"But we have to help those women."

"I'm afraid it's too late." He gently touched her cheek. "But I knew you were the one for me the moment I saw you, even though it took me far too long to admit it. Perhaps it was the same with them."

"I knew it too," she admitted. "Do you really think it might be like that?"

"I hope so. And I promise you that none of my brothers would ever hurt a female."

"I know."

She looked out at the blizzard and sighed, trying to release the tension from her body as she settled back against him. His arms tightened around her in a comforting embrace.

Maybe he was right and maybe, just maybe, those unknown women would end up with their own perfect husbands.

EPILOGUE

A warm summer breeze swept in through the open window as Nelly smiled down at the baby nursing at her breast. Her beautiful, perfect daughter with skin the palest shade of blue and a hint of red in her tiny patch of midnight blue curls.

"She's so beautiful," Artek said, echoing her thoughts as he gently touched their daughter's cheek.

"I understand now," he continued.

"Understand what?"

"How wrong it was to even consider stealing a female from her family. I would kill anyone who tried to take her from us. I should never have let it happen."

"It was their idea, not yours," she reminded him.

"But I didn't stop them."

"Artek, you can't assume responsibility for everything that happens in this world," she said softly. Even though he had come a long way since they first married, he still had a tendency to take the weight of the whole world on his shoulders. "People make mistakes. She'll make mistakes. They won't be your fault. We just have to be there to love her and guide her the best we can."

"If you guide her as successfully as you guide the rest of us, she will have nothing to worry about. I love you, Nelly."

"I love you too." She blinked away tears and smiled up at him.

Voices floated in on the breeze—Artek's brothers and their wives. Their family.

"Everyone is waiting to meet her," he said.

"I know, and I'm happy they're here, but right now, I just want it to be the three of us."

"For as long as you want."

He held her until the baby finished nursing and fell asleep, then helped her adjust her gown and stand up.

"Are you sure this isn't too much for you?"

"I'm sure. And if it is, I'll ask you to bring me back," she promised.

"Thank you."

He kissed her again, and then he opened the doors and they went to join the rest of their family.

AUTHOR'S NOTE

Thank you so much for reading **Artek**! I hope you enjoyed meeting the leader of our alien brothers as much as I enjoyed telling his story! I can't wait to share the adventures of the rest of the brothers with you!

Whether you enjoyed the story or not, it would mean the world to me if you left an honest review on Amazon – reviews are one of the best ways to help other readers find my books!

As usual, I have to thank my readers for coming on these adventures with me - I couldn't do it without you!

And, as always, a special thanks to my beta team – Janet S, Nancy V, and Kitty S. Your thoughts and comments are incredibly helpful!

Up next!

AUTHOR'S NOTE

Seven Brides for Seven Alien Brothers continues with **Benjar!**

Benjar's plan to capture a new bride doesn't turn out exactly the way he intends! What will happen when he has to deal with an impulsive heroine, an isolated cabin, an unexpected snowstorm… and only one bed?

Benjar is available on Amazon!

∼

To make sure you don't miss out on any new releases, please visit my website and sign up for my newsletter!

www.honeyphillips.com

OTHER TITLES

The Alien Abduction Series

Anna and the Alien

Beth and the Barbarian

Cam and the Conqueror

Deb and the Demon

Ella and the Emperor

Faith and the Fighter

Greta and the Gargoyle

Hanna and the Hitman

Izzie and the Icebeast

Joan and the Juggernaut

Kate and the Kraken

Lily and the Lion

Mary and the Minotaur

Nancy and the Naga

Olivia and the Orc

Pandora and the Prisoner

Quinn and the Queller

The Alien Invasion Series
Alien Selection
Alien Conquest
Alien Prisoner
Alien Breeder
Alien Alliance
Alien Hope

Exposed to the Elements
The Naked Alien
The Bare Essentials
A Nude Attitude
The Buff Beast
The Strip Down

Seven Brides for Seven Alien Brothers
Artek
Benjar

Folsom Planet Blues
Alien Most Wanted: Caged Beast
Alien Most Wanted: Prison Mate
Alien Most Wanted: Mastermind
Alien Most Wanted: Unchained

Horned Holidays
Krampus and the Crone
A Gift for Nicholas

Cyborgs on Mars

High Plains Cyborg

The Good, the Bad, and the Cyborg

A Fistful of Cyborg

A Few Cyborgs More

The Magnificent Cyborg

The Outlaw Cyborg

Treasured by the Alien

Mama and the Alien Warrior

A Son for the Alien Warrior

Daughter of the Alien Warrior

A Family for the Alien Warrior

The Nanny and the Alien Warrior

A Home for the Alien Warrior

A Gift for the Alien Warrior

Cosmic Fairy Tales

Jackie and the Giant

Blind Date with an Alien

Her Alien Farmhand

Anthologies

Claimed Among the Stars

Adamant Spirits

Pets in Space 7

ABOUT THE AUTHOR

Honey Phillips writes steamy science fiction stories about hot alien warriors and the human women they can't resist. From abductions to invasions, the ride might be rough, but the end always satisfies.

Honey wrote and illustrated her first book at the tender age of five. Her writing has improved since then. Her drawing skills, unfortunately, have not. She loves writing, reading, traveling, cooking, and drinking champagne - not necessarily in that order.

Honey loves to hear from her wonderful readers! You can stalk her at any of the following locations...

www.facebook.com/HoneyPhillipsAuthor
www.bookbub.com/authors/honey-phillips
www.instagram.com/HoneyPhillipsAuthor
www.honeyphillips.com

Printed in Great Britain
by Amazon